Merry Chistmas Mrs. Sturgen from, Alysssha

Christmas Treasury

FAMILY CLASSIC EDITION

Cover and title page illustrated by Scott Gustafson
Contents page illustrated by Robin Moro
Borders illustrated by Mike Jaroszko
Songs illustrated by Kat Thacker and Marty Noble

PUBLICATIONS INTERNATIONAL, LTD.

CONTENTS

Christmas comes
but once a year,
and when it comes
it brings good cheer.

A CHRISTMAS CAROL

Adapted by Lisa Harkrader
Illustrated by Lydia Halverson

Ebenezer Scrooge hunched over his account books. Scrooge's clerk, Bob Crachit, huddled at his own desk in the tiny outer office. The front door burst open, and a blast of December air whipped through the two rooms.

"Merry Christmas, Uncle!" said Scrooge's nephew, as he strode into the office.

"Christmas," muttered Scrooge. "Bah! Humbug!"

"You can't mean that, Uncle," said his nephew. "Why don't you close early today?"

"And become like other Christmas fools, buying gifts I can't afford?" Scrooge turned back to his books. "No, thank you."

"Suit yourself," said his nephew. "But I hope you'll at least stop by for Christmas dinner tomorrow."

When his nephew opened the door to leave, another gust of wind burst into the office. With it came the sound of carolers singing. Scrooge banged his window open. "You!" he shouted at the carolers. "You there!"

One of the carolers, a young boy, stopped singing and stared up at Scrooge.

"How can a person do an honest day's work with you howling outside his office?" Scrooge snarled. "Find another street corner for your noise. Leave me in peace!"

Scrooge banged the window shut. "Merry Christmas, indeed," he muttered. "What do they have to be merry about?"

"Sir?" Bob Crachit tapped on Scrooge's door. "I've copied all the letters and filed the paperwork. I also brought in more firewood and swept out the ashes. And, well, it's closing time, Mr. Scrooge."

"Fine," said Scrooge. "If your work is finished, you may leave."

"Mr. Scrooge?" said Cratchit. "Tomorrow is Christmas, a day to spend with family."

"You'd like the day off, I suppose?" Scrooge said, as he glared at him.

"Well, yes, Mr. Scrooge," said Cratchit. "After all, it IS Christmas."

"Christmas? Bah!" Scrooge shook his head. "Fine. Take tomorrow off, but be here early the next day."

"Yes, sir. You can count on it, sir," Crachit said, as he pulled his coat snug around him. "Merry Christmas, Mr. Scrooge."

"Humbug," growled Scrooge. He opened the front door, and Crachit scurried out.

At the corner, neighborhood boys were sledding down a steep hill. Crachit leaped headlong onto one of the sleds and slid to the bottom of the hill, laughing and shouting, "Merry Christmas!"

"Fool," Scrooge scowled. He settled back into his chair and finished tallying his accounts.

Darkness fell, and Scrooge closed the last account book. He stood and stretched, his back stiff from the cold and the long hours hunched over his work.

As he locked the countinghouse, he glanced at the sign above the door. It read: THE FIRM OF SCROOGE AND MARLEY.

"Jacob Marley," said Scrooge. "A man who knew the value of a day's work. Too bad he's gone."

Scrooge trudged home, climbed the steps to his bedroom, and huddled in a chair beside the fire to eat his evening gruel.

CLANK! "What the devil?" Scrooge sat still and listened. He heard nothing. "I must have been dreaming." He settled back into his chair.

CLANK! CLANK! Scrooge sat up straight. "That was no dream," he muttered.

"No, it wasn't a dream, Ebenezer." A voice echoed through Scrooge's bedroom. A man, pale and ghostly, drifted into the room.

Scrooge stared at him. "Marley? Jacob Marley? But you're—you're—"

"Dead." The ghost nodded. "And paying for my sins."

"Sins?" Scrooge frowned. "But you were a good man, Jacob. A fine businessman."

"Business? Hah!" Marley's ghost shivered. "Business is meaningless. I never learned the value of love and charity while I was alive. Now I wander the earth, unable to find peace. The same fate awaits you, Ebenezer, unless you change your ways. Three spirits will visit. The first will arrive when the clock strikes one."

The ghost tipped his hat and vanished. Scrooge pulled the covers over his head.

BONG! The clock struck one. "Ebenezer? Ebenezer Scrooge?"

Scrooge peeked out from beneath his sheets. A woman, pale and shimmering, stood beside his bed. In her hand she held a sprig of holly.

"Who are you?" whispered Scrooge.

"I am the Ghost of Christmas Past," said the ghost, as she motioned to the door.

Scrooge crept from his bed and followed the ghost. The room began to dissolve, and soon he was staring into the window of another room, small and dark.

"This house," said Scrooge. "It seems familiar. Why, it's the house I grew up in."

"Yes." The ghost nodded. "And the boy? Is he familiar, too?"

Scrooge peered through the window. A small boy sat alone in the corner, reading a book. Scrooge's eyes grew wide. "It's me as a child! But why am I—why is he—sitting by himself?" Scrooge stared at the boy. "It's Christmas day, isn't it?"

The ghost nodded, then asked, "And where are your parents?"

Scrooge frowned. "Working, I suppose. They worked hard when I was young to give me the things I needed."

"And did they?" asked the ghost. She motioned toward the boy. "Did they give you what you needed?"

Scrooge studied the boy. He looked well-fed and well-dressed, but his eyes were sad and scared. He reminded Scrooge of the caroler from the night before. Then he remembered how he had yelled and frightened the boy.

"We have many places to visit," said the ghost, "and very little time. Come."

The small, dark house faded away, and in its place stood a bright office filled with many workers. "I know this office!" said Scrooge. "I worked here. I was apprenticed to Mr. Fezziwig. Look! There he is."

Scrooge pointed to a gray-haired man carrying a platter of roast beef into the office. Mrs. Fezziwig followed with a tray of pastries. Behind her came house servants carrying bread and pudding and mincemeat pies.

"Stop your work," Mr. Fezziwig told the office clerks. "It's Christmas Eve!"

A fiddler began playing, and Mr. Fezziwig led his wife to the center of the room. He took her in his arms, and they danced a lively jig around the office. The clerks clapped and tapped their feet, and several other couples joined the dance.

The Ghost of Christmas Past glanced at Scrooge. "This certainly isn't the firm of Scrooge and Marley, is it? Do you recognize the clerk in the corner?"

Scrooge stared at the young man. "Me," he whispered. "It's me."

The young Scrooge laughed and clapped to the music. His eyes were bright, his cheeks pink—so different from Scrooge's own clerk, Bob Crachit, who had huddled in the cold the night before, working quietly, his face pale and shadowed.

"I hope this party never ends," young Scrooge called out. "Let's stay and dance forever!"

Old Scrooge thought about Bob Crachit, who had scurried away from the office as quickly as he could on Christmas Eve, never glancing back. "Crachit couldn't wait to get away from me," he said.

The music faded. Fezziwig's office dissolved into darkness.

"We have one more stop," said the ghost. "Our time is running out."

The ghost waved her arms, and Scrooge saw his younger self again, sitting in a garden beside a lovely young woman.

The woman's eyes filled with tears as she said, "I can't marry you, Ebenezer. There's something you love more than me."

"Nonsense," said the young Ebenezer. "I love no other woman."

"That's true." The woman dabbed her eyes with her handkerchief. "You love money. You love it more than anything, and I won't settle for second best."

The woman ran from the garden. Old Scrooge and the ghost followed her.

When she stopped, Scrooge could see that she was a few years older. She was in a parlor that had been brightly decorated for Christmas. Children laughed and played at her feet. A little girl threw her arms around the woman and gave her a kiss.

"Help me tie my bonnet, Mama," said the girl.

Scrooge blinked. "Her children?"

The ghost nodded. "They could have been yours."

The door opened, and a man entered, his arms piled high with gifts.

"Papa!" the children shouted.

They ran to him, hugging his legs. The man laughed and passed out the gifts. Then he pulled his wife into his arms and leaned down to kiss her.

"Stop!" Scrooge clapped his hands over his face. "Take me home! I can't bear it." He collapsed to the floor.

BONG! BONG! The clock struck two. Scrooge blinked. He was back in his own bed. "Thank goodness," he said, as he sank back onto his pillow. "It was a dream."

"No, Ebenezer. It wasn't a dream." A large man, glowing and transparent, stared down at Scrooge. "I am the Ghost of Christmas Present," he said. "I have much to show you. Grab onto my robe." He clapped his filmy hands. "Hurry! We cannot be late."

Scrooge touched the hem of the spirit's robe. The bedroom vanished, and Scrooge found himself on a busy, snowy street. The dark of night had disappeared, and now the morning sun peeked over holly-draped storefronts. Men and women bustled along the sidewalks, while their children laughed and skipped at their sides.

"Everyone looks so happy," grumbled Scrooge.

"Of course they do," said the ghost. "It's Christmas."

Scrooge shook his head. "You mean they all woke up happy, simply because the calendar said December 25?"

The ghost smiled. "Yes. Today they can forget their labors and their troubles, and simply enjoy their families, the fine food on their tables, and the blessings in their lives. When was the last time you stopped and enjoyed the moment, Ebenezer? Try it now. Close your eyes."

Scrooge frowned and closed his eyes. The aroma of freshly baked bread mingled in the crisp morning air. Horses clip-clopped over the cobblestone street. An icy snowflake prickled his tongue, and he realized his mouth had stretched open into a wide smile.

The ghost led Scrooge down the street and into a tiny house. Beside a small Christmas tree, a man was playing with his children—three boys wearing patched trousers and two girls whose dresses were faded and frayed. The man looked up. He was Scrooge's clerk, Bob Crachit.

"Crachit!" Scrooge frowned at the threadbare furnishings. "This is where he lives?"

The ghost nodded. "It's all he can afford. His employer is a bit of a miser. And here's Mrs. Crachit."

A woman carried a small turkey into the dining room on a platter. She had adorned her dress with bright red ribbons, but her dress was mended and worn. She smiled as she carried the platter to the table.

The older children giggled and scrambled to the table.

"Their clothes are rags," said Scrooge, "and their turkey is nothing but bones." He shook his head. "But they're laughing."

Bob Crachit lifted the youngest boy from a chair in the corner and carried him to the table. The boy was pale and thin and carried a crutch.

Scrooge pointed at the boy. "What's wrong with him? Why doesn't he walk?"

"He's very sick," said the ghost. "His name is Tiny Tim, and his parents don't have money for a doctor. If the future remains unchanged, Tiny Tim will die."

"Die?" Scrooge stared at the boy.

Tiny Tim raised his cup of water and smiled at his mother and father. "Merry Christmas!" he said. "God bless us every one."

"Come," said the ghost, and he turned to leave.

"But the boy," said Scrooge. "Tiny Tim. There must be something we can do."

"Perhaps," said the ghost, as he led Scrooge from the house. Outside, the street was gone, and Scrooge found himself watching another family—a mother, father, grandparents, and children, celebrating Christmas in a hut.

Scrooge frowned and said, "They're sitting on a dirt floor, eating from crude bowls, yet they're laughing."

The hut vanished and was replaced by a tiny lighthouse room. The lighthouse keeper and his assistant were sharing Christmas dinner at a rickety wooden table. Outside, waves crashed against the rocks.

"Bless this day," said the lighthouse keeper.

As the two men lifted their mugs in a toast, the lighthouse faded. Scrooge found himself entering another dining room, one Scrooge knew very well.

"My nephew's house!" said Scrooge. "He's having a party."

The party guests were taking turns imitating well-known people—the queen, the prime minister, a famous actress.

Scrooge's nephew stood up and said, "Guess who I am?" He pulled coins from his pocket, counted them, counted them again, then clutched them tight in his fist and muttered, "Christmas. Humbug."

"Easy," shouted a man. "Ebenezer Scrooge!" The other guests laughed.

"They're making fun of me," said Scrooge.

The ghost nodded. "And they always will. Unless the future changes."

"Change? But how?" cried Scrooge.

BONG! BONG! BONG! Scrooge blinked. He was in his own bed again, and the Ghost of Christmas Present was gone. But as he sat up, another ghost floated into the room. He was draped in black, and a dark hood hid his face.

Scrooge pulled the sheets to his chin. "Who are you?" he asked.

The phantom said nothing.

"First came the Ghost of Christmas Past, then the Ghost of Christmas Present," Scrooge said, as he stared at the phantom. "You must be the Ghost of Christmas Yet to Come. Are you here to show me the future and how it can change?"

The phantom gestured toward the door. Scrooge followed him to the street in front of his countinghouse. The door was locked, and the windows were dark. Three men stood out front, talking and shaking their heads.

"I know those fellows," said Scrooge. "I do business with them. We're quite friendly. These men like me, even if my own nephew does not."

The ghost led Scrooge closer. Scrooge could hear what the men were saying.

"Poor old Scrooge," said one. "They say he's very sick."

"He must be near dead if he's closed up his firm for the day," said another.

"If I know Ebenezer," said the third man, "he'll work during his own funeral."

The men laughed. "It is bad news, though," said the first man. "If Scrooge closes down, I'll have to find another countinghouse."

"Another countinghouse!" sputtered Scrooge. "But I'm not closing down." He turned to the ghost. "Why did you bring me here?"

The phantom turned and drifted down the street. Scrooge followed him and soon found himself in a tiny room with faded walls and worn furnishings.

"But this is Crachit's house," Scrooge said, as he peered around the room. "I've already been here. I've already seen them."

The spirit shook his head and led Scrooge into a bedroom that was hardly bigger than a closet. Mr. Crachit sat next to a small bed and held Tiny Tim's hand. Tears trickled down Mr. Crachit's cheeks.

"What's wrong with them?" said Scrooge. "They were so happy last time I was here, laughing and playing. And where's Mrs. Crachit?"

The bedroom door opened, and Mrs. Crachit came in. Scrooge watched Tiny Tim sleeping in the bed. He was thinner than he had been at Christmas dinner, and his face was drawn and pale. His crutch rested against the bed, and a ball of mistletoe hung above his head.

"Did you see Scrooge?" asked Mrs. Crachit. "Will the old miser help us?"

Bob Crachit shook his head. "Mr. Scrooge says he won't help those who can't help themselves." He took Mrs. Cratchit's hand in his. "But Mr. Scrooge's nephew offered to help us."

Tiny Tim's eyes fluttered open. "Mr. Scrooge's nephew will help? Bless him."

"I pray it's not too late," said Mrs. Crachit. "We can't go on without Tiny Tim."

"Without Tiny Tim?" Scrooge turned toward the ghost. "But that can't be. He's not dying, is he?"

The ghost nodded and turned toward the door. He motioned for Scrooge to follow.

"No!" cried Scrooge. "We can't leave. We must help him."

The ghost drifted from the room. The Crachits' house faded, and Scrooge found himself outside. Clouds filled the sky, and an icy wind whipped through the trees. Scrooge glanced around. A gravel path led through rows of granite stones.

"Why, this is a cemetery," said Scrooge. He stared at the ghost. "Oh, no. Not Tiny Tim. Don't tell me you've come here to show me his grave. It can't be too late."

The ghost pointed at a new grave. A priest stood alone, praying. When the prayer was finished, the priest turned and strode away.

"Is this the grave we came to see?" Scrooge frowned. "But where are the Crachits? And the other mourners? Why did no one come to the funeral?"

The ghost motioned toward the headstone. Scrooge squinted. Engraved on it were two words: EBENEZER SCROOGE.

Scrooge stared. "Mine," he whispered. "The grave is mine." He turned to the ghost. "This is the future?"

The ghost nodded.

Scrooge closed his eyes. "Now I understand. I understand what you have been trying to tell me." He fell to his knees. "You must give me another chance. I will live in the past, the present, and the future."

"I will live in the past, the present, and the future! I will live in the past, the present, and the future!" Scrooge cried again and again.

He opened his eyes. He was in his own room again. The spirit was gone.

"Oh, thank you!" Scrooge scrambled from his bed. "I've been given another chance. And I WILL live in the past, present, and future." Scrooge flung open his window. The aroma of freshly baked bread drifted on the crisp morning air and into his room. Horses clip-clopped over the cobblestone street.

"You! You there!" he shouted to a boy on the street. "What day is this?"

The boy gave Scrooge a puzzled look. "It's Christmas, sir. Christmas morning."

"Good! I haven't missed it. Here, lad." Scrooge rummaged in his dresser drawer and pulled out a bag of money. He tossed a handful of coins to the boy and said, "There's a big, juicy turkey in the butcher shop window at the end of the street. Buy it and deliver it to Bob Crachit's house."

The boy held up the coins. "But, sir. You've given me too much. This is twice what the turkey will cost."

"Keep the rest for your trouble. Hurry now. The Crachits are hungry."

The boy grinned. "Yes, sir!" He scurried away down the street.

"Oh! Young fellow?" Scrooge called after him.

The boy turned. "Yes, sir?"

"Have a merry Christmas," said Scrooge.

"Thank you, sir," said the boy. "And merry Christmas to you, too."

Scrooge dressed in his finest clothes, planted his top hat snugly on his head, and set off down the busy, snowy street toward his nephew's house. Everything looked very familiar to Scrooge. "It's just like before," he said, "when the Ghost of Christmas Present showed me the street on Christmas morning."

He tipped his hat to a group of carolers and waved to a coachman who drove past. A family hurried down the street toward the church, and Scrooge stopped to pat their young son on the head.

"Here, young fellow," Scrooge said. He reached into his pocket, pulled out a penny, and handed it to the boy. "Buy yourself some Christmas candy."

The boy stared at the coin. "Thank you, sir."

"Merry Christmas," said Scrooge.

"Merry Christmas to you," said the boy's mother. "And God bless you."

When Scrooge reached his nephew's house, his nephew was surprised to see him. "Uncle!" he cried. "Did you change your mind about Christmas dinner? Have you come to celebrate the holiday with us?"

"Yes," said Scrooge. "If you will have me."

"Of course we'll have you!" said his nephew.

His nephew took Scrooge's hat and coat and led him into the dining room, where his wife set an extra place at the table.

"We're so glad you could join us," she said. "You've arrived just in time to carve the turkey."

After dinner, Scrooge pushed his chair back from the table. "Thank you," he said. "I've never eaten a more delicious meal. I hate to leave so soon, but I have another stop to make, and I can't be late."

He donned his coat and hat, and hurried down the street to Bob Crachit's house. The Crachits were surprised to see him.

"Oh, Mr. Scrooge!" said Mrs. Crachit. "How can we ever thank you for this wonderful turkey?"

Scrooge smiled. "By enjoying every bite," he said. Scrooge turned to her husband. "Crachit, you've worked long hours without complaining for many years. It's time I gave you a raise, don't you think?"

"Why, yes! Thank you, sir," said Bob Crachit. "You're so generous."

"Nonsense," said Scrooge. "I should have done it years ago. I promise I won't make you wait so long for your next raise."

Scrooge kept his promise, too. He raised Bob Crachit's salary and made sure Tiny Tim got the very best medical treatment. Tiny Tim grew tall and strong, and he told people that Mr. Scrooge had become a second father to him.

Everyone said Ebenezer Scrooge was the only man who knew how to keep Christmas all year long. He draped his office in pine and holly, gave money to the poor, and sang Christmas carols even in July.

And each time he sat down to a meal with his friends and family, he would raise his glass in a toast. "God bless us," he would say. "God bless us every one."

I am the Christmas Spirit!
I cause the aged to renew their youth,
and to laugh in the old, glad way.
I keep romance alive in the heart of
childhood, and brighten sleep with
dreams of woven magic.

I cause eager feet to climb dark
stairways with filled baskets,
leaving behind hearts amazed at the
goodness of the world.

E.C. Baird

God Rest Ye Merry Gentlemen

London

Vigorously

1.God rest ye mer - ry gen - tle - men, Let noth - ing ye dis - may. Re -
2.From God our heav'n - ly fa - ther, A bless - ed An - gel came, And

mem - ber Christ our Sa - viour was born on Christ - mas day. To
un - to cer - tain shep - herds brought tid - ings of the same. How

3. The shepherds at those tidings
   Rejoiced much in mind
   And left their flocks a-feeding
   In tempest, storm, and wind,
   And went straightway to Bethlehem
   The Son of God to find.
   O tidings, etc.

4. And when they came to Bethlehem,
   Where our dear Saviour lay,
   They found Him in a manger
   Where oxen feed on hay;
   His Mother Mary kneeling down
   Unto the Lord did pray.
   O tidings, etc.

CHRISTMAS IN

England

Written by Sarah Toast   Illustrated by Robert Y. Larsen

It is cold, wet, and foggy in England at Christmastime. Families welcome the warmth and cheer of a Yule log blazing on the hearth. They decorate their homes with holly, ivy, and other evergreens and hang a mistletoe "kissing bough."

Throughout the holidays, carolers go from house to house at twilight ringing handbells and singing Christmas songs. "The Holly and the Ivy" and "Hark! The Herald Angels Sing" are English favorites. People give the carolers treats, such as little pies filled with nuts and dried fruits.

The day before Christmas is very busy for families in England. They wrap presents, bake cookies, and hang stockings over the fireplace. Then everyone gathers around the tree as someone tells the favorite story, "A Christmas Carol."

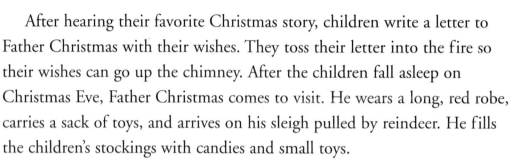

After hearing their favorite Christmas story, children write a letter to Father Christmas with their wishes. They toss their letter into the fire so their wishes can go up the chimney. After the children fall asleep on Christmas Eve, Father Christmas comes to visit. He wears a long, red robe, carries a sack of toys, and arrives on his sleigh pulled by reindeer. He fills the children's stockings with candies and small toys.

On Christmas Day, everyone sits down to the midday feast and finds a colorful Christmas cracker beside their dinner plate. A Christmas cracker is a paper-covered tube. When the end tabs are pulled, there is a loud crack. Out spills a paper hat to wear at dinner, small trinkets, and a riddle to read aloud to everyone at the table.

The family enjoys a feast of turkey with chestnut stuffing, roast goose with currants, or roast beef and Yorkshire pudding. Brussel sprouts are likely to be the vegetables. Best of all is the plum pudding topped with a sprig of holly. Brandy is poured over the plum pudding and set aflame. Then family members enjoy a dramatic show as it is carried into the dining room. Whoever finds the silver charm baked in their serving has good luck the following year. The wassail bowl, brimming with hot, spiced wine, tops off the day's feast. It is said that all quarrels stop when people drink wassail.

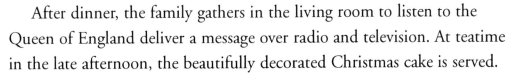

After dinner, the family gathers in the living room to listen to the Queen of England deliver a message over radio and television. At teatime in the late afternoon, the beautifully decorated Christmas cake is served.

The day after Christmas is called Boxing Day. This day has nothing to do with fighting. Long ago, people filled church alms boxes with donations for the poor. Then on December 26, the boxes were distributed. Now people often use this day to give small gifts of money to the mail carrier, news vendor, and others who have helped them during the year.

Beginning on Boxing Day, families can enjoy stage performances called pantomimes. This activity originally meant a play without words, or actors who mimed or entertained without speaking. Pantomime now refers to all kinds of plays performed during the Christmas season. Such familiar children's stories as "Cinderella" and "Peter Pan" delight young and old alike.

In some towns, masked and costumed performers called mummers present plays or sing carols in the streets.

A CHRISTMAS MIRACLE

Written by Lisa Harkrader
Illustrated by Kathleen McCord

Rose rubbed the sleeve of her nightgown against the frosty glass and peered out into the night sky. The moon peeked over the mountain behind the little cabin.

Rose searched the sky. She needed to find a shooting star. Christmas was only three days away, and she had to make a wish.

"Rose McKenzie, stop your daydreaming," Mama said. She pulled the curtain shut and kissed the top of Rose's head. "It's time for bed."

Rose scrubbed her face and hands in the washbasin and ran a brush through her tangled hair. Her brothers, James and Henry, were settling down on their mattresses near the fire. Baby Bonnie was already fast asleep in her little bed—a drawer lined with soft blankets that rested on the chair beside her parents' bed.

Rose leaned over to kiss the baby good-night. Then she kissed Mama and Papa, blew out the lantern, and crawled into the little fold-up bed next to the window that she shared with her sister, Sarah.

Rose tugged the covers to her chin. The fire in the fireplace hissed and popped. Papa's snores rattled through the cabin. Outside, the wind rustled through the trees.

And Rose thought she would never fall asleep. It was too close to Christmas, too close to the most wonderful day of the year, and too close to the morning when her family would open small homemade gifts again.

Rose looked out the window again. She remembered how Mama had stared at the lacy green dress in the window of Mr. Pranger's store when they drove into town. Rose wanted to give her mama that dress.

She closed her eyes and could see Mama opening it on Christmas morning.

There was Mama, laughing out loud in surprise. The green lace dress matched Mama's sparkling green eyes.

Then Papa opened his gift—a shiny black pipe. Not a homemade one, whittled from a hickory branch. A brand-new pipe ordered from a catalog and shipped all the way from New York City.

Bonnie's gift was a crib, carved and painted, and the boys got new wool coats. In Sarah's gift was a note that said, "Look outside." Sarah pulled open the door, and there stood a dapple gray pony with a big red ribbon around his neck.

"They got just what they wanted," Rose murmured.

She opened her eyes. Sunlight streamed into the cabin.

Rose shook her head. "It was only a dream," Rose said, as she smiled. "But what a wonderful dream. I wish it could come true."

After breakfast, Rose helped her mother wash dishes. "Mama," she said. "If you could have anything for Christmas, anything at all, what would you wish for?"

Mama smiled and set the clean plates in the cupboard. "I already have everything I could want—you, your brothers and sisters, and your father, all in good health."

"I know, but I mean something extra," Rose said, as she squeezed out the dish towel. "Something wrapped in a box that you could open on Christmas morning. What would it be?"

"Well, it would be a mighty funny-looking box," said Mama. "But if I could have something extra, I'd wish for a Christmas tree, tall and full, with so many decorations you could hardly see the branches. And a big, plump turkey I could roast with dressing and potatoes." She leaned against the cupboard and smiled. "And when it was done, we would sit down at the table next to our Christmas tree, and eat the finest Christmas dinner any of us have ever tasted." She closed her eyes. "I can almost taste it now."

"And a new dress?" asked Rose. "Would you like a new dress?"

"Yes," Mama nodded. "A new dress." Then she shook her head. "But there's no sense wishing for something you can't have."

Papa chuckled. "Looks like Rose isn't the only dreamer in the family." He reached for his rifle. "I can't promise you a turkey, but maybe I can find a fat goose for our Christmas dinner."

He pulled on his coat and headed toward the woods.

Rose waited for Papa all morning. While she swept the cabin, peeled potatoes, and mended her stockings, she kept peeking out the window to see if Papa would bring home a goose.

Finally, just before noon, Papa tramped out of the woods carrying a gunnysack over his shoulder. Rose threw down her mending and burst out the door.

"Papa, you did it!" she cried. "We'll have roast goose for Christmas after all."

Papa laughed. "Not quite, missy." He opened the sack. "I didn't see any geese, but I did bring home a pheasant big enough to feed seven hungry McKenzies."

Papa hung the pheasant under the eaves outside the cabin. Its russet and green feathers gleamed in the sunlight.

"I'll need to clean it," Papa said. He blew on his hands and rubbed them together. "First I need to go inside and warm up. Is that your mama's potato soup I smell?"

Rose followed Papa inside and helped Mama ladle out seven bowls of soup. While they ate, Rose tried to watch the pheasant. But every time she glanced out the window, Papa said, "Eat your soup."

After lunch, Rose ran to the window and shouted, "Oh, no! Papa, look. He's eating our Christmas dinner!"

Rose pointed at a bear that had wandered into the yard and pulled the pheasant down from the eaves.

Papa flung open the door. The bear ran off into the woods. All that remained were a few russet feathers lying in the grass.

The next day was Christmas Eve. After breakfast, Papa, Henry, and James pulled on their boots and coats and set out for the woods.

"Don't worry," Papa said. "We'll have a fine Christmas dinner yet."

Rose waited by the window. Sarah came and sat down beside her. The sun rose high in the sky. Finally Papa and the boys hiked out of the woods. James carried a gunnysack over his shoulder.

Rose and Sarah rushed to the door, and Rose flung it open.

"Did you get another pheasant?" Rose asked.

"Is it as big as the first one?" asked Sarah.

"Not a pheasant," said Papa, "and not as big."

James opened the sack and pulled out a small quail. "Birds just aren't that plentiful this time of year," said Papa. "But we won't leave this one under the eaves." He laughed and said, "That pesky bear can catch his own Christmas dinner." Papa and the boys cleaned the quail right away and brought it into the house.

Rose stared at the little bird. "But this can't be our dinner," she said. "It's barely enough to feed Bonnie."

"Nonsense," said Mama. Then she kissed Papa on the cheek. "It's exactly enough. Rose, you can help me peel potatoes, carrots, and onions for quail soup. And Sarah, you can help me bake loaves of bread. Then you can both take turns churning fresh butter. This will be the finest meal we've eaten in months."

Mama pulled her big soup kettle from the cupboard and put it on the stove.

The quail soup simmered, and the bread dough baked into crusty brown loaves. Savory aromas filled the cabin. Rose and Sarah churned butter until they were sure their arms would fall off.

Finally, as the sun sank over the mountaintop, Mama said, "Help me set the table, Henry. Dinner's ready."

Sarah and James scrambled to their chairs. Rose placed the bread in the center of the table, and Henry set out bowls and spoons. Mama carried the hot soup over from the stove, and Papa held Bonnie in his arms. Then they all bowed their heads to give thanks.

Tap. Tap. Rose looked up. Someone was knocking at the cabin door.

Mama frowned at Papa and said, "Who would be visiting way out here at this time of night?"

Tap. Tap. Papa opened the door. A stranger stood on the step. His eyelids sagged with weariness.

The stranger's voice quivered. "Could you shelter a hungry traveler from the cold?"

"Of course," Papa said. He opened the door for the stranger. "You're just in time for dinner. We don't have much, but you are welcome to share what we have."

"Bless you," said the stranger. "Merry Christmas."

Mama set an extra place at the table and began ladling out the soup. When she finished filling the eighth bowl—the stranger's bowl—the soup kettle was empty. "Look at that," Mama said. She set the bowl in front of the stranger. "We have just enough."

After dinner, the stranger helped clear the table, then sat in a chair by the fire.

"Where did you come from?" Sarah asked him.

The man chuckled. "I've traveled for so long, it's hard to say just where I'm from. I've been to the Great Lakes and to New York City and to the White House. I've even met Abraham Lincoln himself."

Henry's eyes grew wide. "Abraham Lincoln!" he exclaimed.

The stranger nodded. "Twice. I plan to keep traveling and meeting good folks like yourselves. I want to see the ocean someday, and the Grand Canyon."

"And the giant redwoods?" asked James.

"And the giant redwoods," said the stranger. He pulled a harmonica from his pocket and began playing. Papa pushed the table aside and pulled Rose to the center of the floor. Sarah picked up Bonnie, Mama grabbed the boys, and soon everyone was dancing.

The stranger played and played, and Rose's family danced and danced. Finally, Mama collapsed in a chair. "Time for bed," she said.

James and Henry piled blankets on the floor by the fire for the stranger, and everyone crawled into bed.

Before Rose closed her eyes, she took one more look out the window. A bright yellow star shot across the sky, leaving a sparkling trail behind it. "Oh!" she cried. Rose stared at the shooting star. "Please let my family have a wonderful Christmas," she whispered, "and let Mama have a Christmas tree."

Dawn peeked over the mountain. Rose opened her eyes. It was Christmas! She would surprise her parents and the traveling stranger by making the coffee before anyone else awoke.

She tiptoed toward the fire. James and Henry were fast asleep, and the stranger was gone! On the floor where he had slept lay a bulging gunnysack.

"Mama! Papa!" Rose shouted. "Look."

Her parents rushed over, Sarah stumbled out of bed, and the boys sat up on their mattresses. They all stared at the sack.

"It's filled with presents," Papa said. He pulled out a box and read the tag. "This one's for you, Sarah, and this one's for Mama."

He passed out the gifts, then he, Mama, Sarah, and the boys began pulling off wrapping paper. Mama lifted a green lace dress from her box, and Papa opened a shiny, new pipe. James and Henry unwrapped new wool coats, Sarah unwrapped a toy horse, and Mama helped baby Bonnie unwrap the biggest gift of all—a crib, carved and painted, just like in Rose's dream.

Rose watched in silence. She was happy for her family. Still, the sack was empty, and there was no gift for her. She ran to the window to hide her tears.

"Oh!" she cried. "Look!"

Outside stood a fir tree, full and tall, with beautiful hand-carved decorations. Rose ran out the door. On the tree was a note that said: "To Rose. Merry Christmas."

"It's a miracle!" she shouted. "My wish came true. Merry Christmas!"

THE FIRST CHRISTMAS TREE

Written by Suzanne Lieurance
Illustrated by John Lund

Papa shook the snow from his scarf as he entered the doorway of his warm and cozy little house. Once inside he laid a small pine tree next to the door.

Gretchen's face lit up when she spotted the tree. "Papa! Our Christmas tree?"

Papa pulled off his scarf and coat. "Yes, this is our Christmas tree," he said.

Gretchen's eyes sparkled. "Where shall we put it?" she asked.

Mama looked up from the table where she was working with bits of colored paper, apples, and wafers.

Gretchen danced around the room. "It's almost Christmas," she said. "Shouldn't we decorate the tree?"

"Of course," said Mama. "Help me with these cuttings."

Gretchen plopped down at the table. Mama patiently showed her how to shape colored paper into beautiful hearts, roses, flowers, angels, and bells. Papa warmed himself by the fire as Mama and Gretchen fashioned lots of lovely, delicate ornaments.

"Why do we have Christmas trees?" asked Gretchen. "Who had the first one?"

Papa rubbed his beard as he spoke. "It's a custom. A custom that started long, long ago, right here in Germany."

"The first Christmas trees were not decorated at all," said Mama. "And they weren't pine trees."

"That's right," said Papa. "Long, long ago, in the 700's, a monk named Boniface chopped down an oak tree. He was angry because people thought the oak was sacred, and he wanted to show them they were wrong."

Gretchen frowned. "So an oak was the first Christmas tree?" she asked.

"No, no," said Mama. "Let Papa finish his story."

"When the oak fell, it crushed everything in its path," said Papa. "Everything, that is, except a small fir sapling. Boniface said the survival of the little sapling was a miracle. So, for many years after, people planted fir saplings to celebrate Christmas. They didn't bring trees inside and decorate them as we do now."

Mama stood up. "And now it's time to decorate this tree," she said.

Papa lifted the little pine onto the table by the window. Then he and Mama hung all the pretty paper cuttings, along with bright red apples and delicate wafers, from the pine's spindly branches.

When they finished, Gretchen stood back to admire it all. "What a beautiful custom," she said. Then she knelt before the window, folded her hands, and looked toward the sky. "Thank you, Boniface, for giving us that very first Christmas tree."

Here We Come A-Caroling

England

3. We are not daily beggars
   That beg from door to door,
   But we are neighbors' children
   Whom you have seen before.
   Love and joy, etc.

4. God bless the master of this house,
   Likewise the mistress too,
   And all the little children
   That round the table go.
   Love and joy, etc.

THE FIRST CHRISTMAS TREE LIGHTS

Written by Suzanne Lieurance
Illustrated by Jane Maday

It was a cold winter's afternoon in the dense German forest. Martin Luther did not notice the sun slowly setting and the sky growing dark. His thoughts were on the sermon he was preparing. The forest soon came alive with the night sounds of owls, wolves, and other wild creatures.

Martin Luther shivered. He pulled his cloak tighter around his shoulders. Then he quickened his pace, saying a little prayer for comfort as he went.

The forest grew darker. Martin Luther scurried along, continuing to pray that he would not cross paths with a wild animal. He glanced up to see the night sky filled with tiny pricks of light, twinkling blue and silver. What could they be?

"Stars!" Martin Luther said suddenly, as he realized what he was seeing. "Lights from Heaven to guide and comfort me, just as a star led the Wise Men to the stable that first Christmas. What a splendid theme for my sermon."

Martin Luther smiled up at the twinkling sky. He was no longer afraid.

Feeling safer, Martin Luther looked around for a small tree he could take home for Christmas. He found a young fir tree, pulled it up, and dragged it with him through the forest.

At long last Martin Luther was safe at home. He quickly prepared the little fir tree, hoping to surprise his family.

"Hmmm," he said, as he noticed the triangle shaped candle holder on the table by the window.

Soon Martin Luther called his family in, so he could tell them about his long walk through the dark and dangerous forest. Everyone gasped at the sight of the little fir tree, for it was customary to hang Christmas trees upside-down from the ceiling beams and leave them undecorated. Yet, Martin Luther had placed this little tree upright in a pot, high on the table. The candles had been removed from the triangle shaped holder. Now, as the very first Christmas tree lights, they flickered from the tree's delicate branches—just as the stars had flickered through the forest to guide Martin Luther.

The family gathered around as Martin Luther told them what had happened earlier that evening.

"Just as I was getting very frightened, I saw the stars twinkling through the trees as if God was saying, 'Don't be afraid, for I am with you.' And that's when I realized the theme for my sermon. God's light shines through the darkest night for everyone, but sometimes we have to look up to see it."

O Christmas Tree

Germany

2. O Christmas tree, O Christmas tree,
   Much pleasure doth thou bring me.
   For every year the Christmas tree,
   Brings to us all both joy and glee.
   O Christmas tree, O Christmas tree,
   Much pleasure doth thou bring me.

3. O Christmas tree, O Christmas tree,
   Thy candles shine out brightly.
   Each bough doth hold its tiny light,
   That makes each toy to sparkle bright.
   O Christmas tree, O Christmas tree,
   Thy candles shine out brightly.

THE STORY OF CHRISTMAS SPIDERS

Written by Stephanie Herbek
Illustrated by Jane Maday

In a quiet cottage in the woods lived a gentle widow and her eight children. The widow worked very hard to keep her children warm and well-fed, but money was not plentiful. When the air grew crisp, and the snow began to fall, the widow knew Christmas was coming. But instead of feeling joyful as the holiday approached, she felt sadness and sorrow. She knew that she did not have enough money to buy her children any gifts to open on Christmas morning.

"I cannot afford new toys or books," she thought, walking home through the woods one night. "What will I give my children?"

On Christmas Eve the family ate their simple Christmas dinner together, and the widow tried to conceal her worries. After tucking her excited children snugly into bed, she pulled her chair close to the fire and tried to erase the visions of their little disappointed faces from her mind. After all, what fun is Christmas morning without gifts to open?

"Perhaps a Christmas tree would make my children happy," the widow sighed. She put on her coat and hat and walked through the woods in search of the right tree. She chose a small but beautiful evergreen, chopped it down with her husband's ax, and brought it to the cottage. For hours, the widow carefully decorated the fragrant tree branches with colorful fruits, bits of ribbon, and Christmas cookies. Then she blew out her candle and went to bed, hoping the tree would make her children's empty Christmas a little bit brighter.

While the tired widow slept, tiny spiders crept from the cracks and corners of the cottage. They had watched her hard at work, decorating the tree for her children. Onto the branches they jumped, spinning delicate strands of silky web which gracefully covered the small tree from trunk to top. It was a beautiful sight.

When the family awoke on Christmas morning, they could not believe their eyes. The webs of silk had been turned into pure silver, covering the tree with dazzling brightness! During the night, Santa Claus had come with gifts for the children and saw the tree covered with spiderwebs. He smiled as he saw how happy the spiders were, but knew how heartbroken the widow would be if she saw her tree covered with spiderwebs. So he turned the silky webs into pure, shining silver. The next morning, as the widow watched her children sing and dance around the beautiful shining tree, she knew it would be a wonderful Christmas after all!

From that day forward, people have hung strands of shiny silver tinsel on their Christmas trees in honor of the poor widow and her tiny Christmas spiders.

O Little Town of Bethlehem

Words: Phillips Brooks

Music: Lewis H. Redner

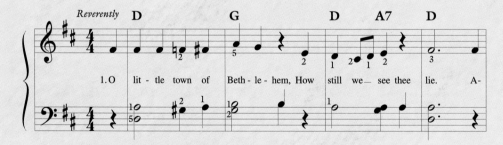

1.O lit - tle town of Beth - le - hem, How still we — see thee lie. A-

bove thy deep and dream- less sleep, The si - lent— stars go by. Yet

in thy dark streets shin - eth The e - ver - last - ing light. The

hopes and fears of all the years Are met in— thee to - night.

2. For Christ is born of Mary,
   And gathered all above.
   While mortals sleep, the angels keep
   Their watch of wond'ring love.
   O morning stars, together
   Proclaim the holy birth,
   And praises sing to God the King,
   And peace to men on earth.

3. How silently how silently
   The wondrous gift is given.
   So God imparts to human hearts
   The blessing of His heaven.
   No ear may hear His coming,
   But in this world of sin,
   Where meek souls will receive Him still,
   The dear Christ enters in.

The First Christmas

Luke 2:1-16

Illustrated by Crista C. Abvabi

And it came to pass in those days, that there went out a decree from Caesar Augustus, that all the world should be taxed.

(And this taxing was first made when Cyrenius was governor of Syria.)

And all went to be taxed, everyone into his own city.

And Joseph also went up from Galilee, out of the city of Nazareth, into Judea, unto the city of David, which is called Bethlehem; (because he was of the house and lineage of David):

To be taxed with Mary his espoused wife, being great with child.

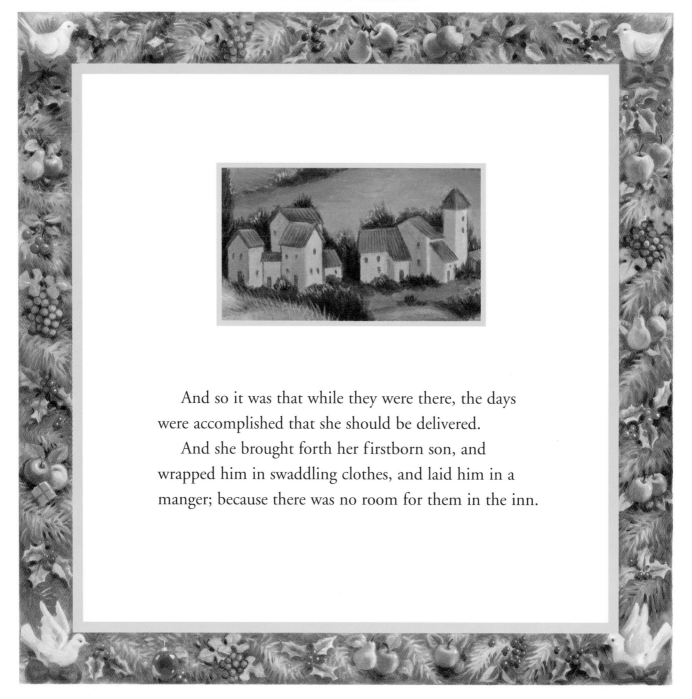

And so it was that while they were there, the days were accomplished that she should be delivered.

And she brought forth her firstborn son, and wrapped him in swaddling clothes, and laid him in a manger; because there was no room for them in the inn.

And there were in the same country
shepherds abiding in the field, keeping watch
over their flock by night.

And lo, the angel of the Lord came upon them, and the glory of the Lord shone round about them: and they were sore afraid.

And the angel said unto them, Fear not: for, behold, I bring you good tidings of great joy, which shall be to all people.

For unto you is born this day in the city of David a Saviour, which is Christ the Lord.

And this shall be a sign unto you; Ye shall find the babe wrapped in swaddling clothes, lying in a manger.

And suddenly there was with the angel a multitude of the heavenly host praising God, and saying,

Glory to God in the highest, and on earth peace, good will toward men.

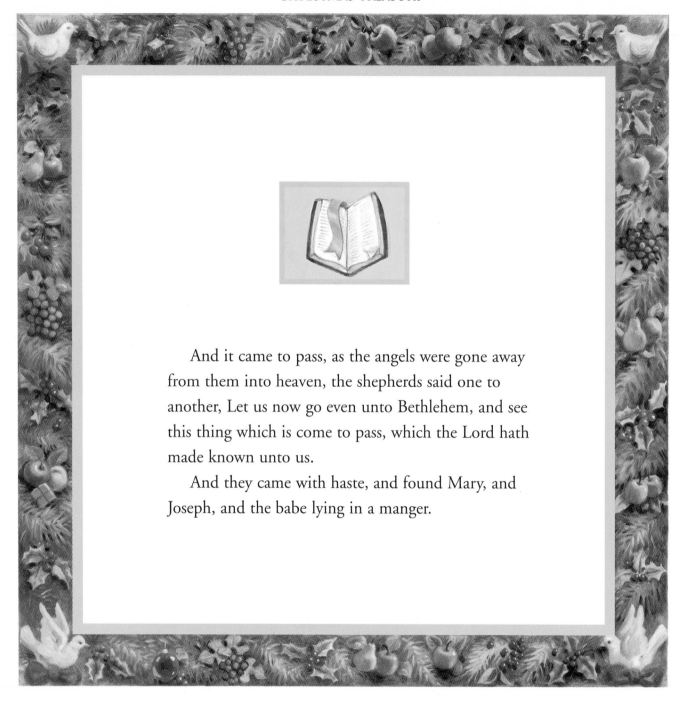

And it came to pass, as the angels were gone away from them into heaven, the shepherds said one to another, Let us now go even unto Bethlehem, and see this thing which is come to pass, which the Lord hath made known unto us.

And they came with haste, and found Mary, and Joseph, and the babe lying in a manger.

While Shepherds Watched Their Flocks

George Frederick Handel

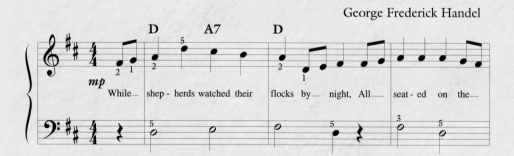

While— shep - herds watched their flocks by— night, All— seat - ed on the—

ground,_____ The____ an - gel of the Lord came__ down, And____

glo - ry shone a - round,_____ And glo - ry shone a - round.

2. "Fear not," said he; for mighty dread
   Had seized their trouble mind;
   "Glad tidings of great joy I bring
   To you and all mankind."

3. "To you in David's town this day
   Is born of David's line
   A Savior, who is Christ the Lord;
   And this shall be the sign."

4. "The heavenly Babe you there shall find
   To human view displayed,
   All meanly wrapped in swathing bands,
   And in a manger laid."

5. Thus spake the seraph; and forthwith
   Appeared a shining throng
   Of angels praising God, who thus
   Addressed their joyful song.

O Come All Ye Faithful

Latin: J. Reading
English translation: Rev. F. Oakeley

Traditional

2. Sing, choirs of angels, sing in exultation,
Sing, all ye citizens of heav'n above.
Glory to God, glory in the highest,
O come, etc.

3. Yea Lord, we greet Thee, born this happy morning,
Jesus, to Thee be glory giv'n.
Word of the Father, now in flesh appearing.
O come, etc.

The Friendly Beasts

Illustrated by Linda Dockey Graves

Jesus, our brother, strong and good,

Was humbly born in a stable rude,

And the friendly beasts around Him stood,

Jesus, our brother, strong and good.

"I," said the donkey, shaggy and brown,
"I carried His mother uphill and down,
I carried her safely to Bethlehem town;
I," said the donkey, shaggy and brown.

"I," said the cow, all white and red,
"I gave Him my manger for His bed,
I gave Him my hay to pillow His head;
I," said the cow, all white and red.

"I," said the sheep with curly horn,
"I gave Him my wool for His blanket warm,
He wore my coat on Christmas morn;
I," said the sheep, with curly horn.

"I," said the dove, from the rafters high,
"Cooed Him to sleep, my mate and I,
We cooed Him to sleep, my mate and I;
I," said the dove, from the rafters high.

And every beast, by some good spell,
In the stable dark was glad to tell,
Of the gift he gave Immanuel,
The gift he gave Immanuel.

Joy to the World

Words: Isaac Watts   Music: George F. Handel

1. Joy to the world, The Lord is come, Let earth re-ceive her King, Let

Hark! The Herald Angels Sing

Words: Charles Wesley

Music: Felix Mendelssohn

2. Christ by highest heav'n adored,
   Christ the everlasting Lord!
   Late in time behold Him come,
   Offspring of a virgin's womb.
   Veiled in flesh the Godhead see,
   Hail the Incarnate Deity,
   Pleased with men as man to dwell,
   Jesus our Immanuel!
   Hark! The herald angels sing
   Glory to the newborn King.

3. Hail, the heav'n-born Prince of Peace!
   Hail, the Son of Righteousness!
   Life and light to all He brings,
   Ris'n with healing in His wings.
   Mild He lays His glory by,
   Born that man no more may die,
   Born to raise the sons of earth,
   Born to give them second birth.
   Hark! The herald angels sing
   Glory to the newborn King.

CHRISTMAS IN
Italy

Written by Sarah Toast

Illustrated by Mike Jaroszko

The Christmas season begins in Italy on the first Sunday of Advent, which is four Sundays before Christmas. In the cold winter weather of the northern mountains and in the mild weather of the south, Christmas fairs feature fireworks and bonfires along with holiday music. Families go to the Christmas markets to shop for gifts and new figures for the manger scene. Some families set up a Christmas tree and decorate it.

During novena, the nine days before and including Christmas Day, children go from house to house reciting Christmas verses for coins. The family sets up its *presepio,* or manger scene, on the first day of the novena. They gather before the *presepio* each morning or evening of novena to light candles and pray.

Some families put life-size figures of Mary and Joseph in their front yard. Both manger scenes and Christmas carols originated in Italy.

During this time, children write letters to their parents wishing them a merry Christmas, promising good behavior, and making a list of the gifts they hope to receive. The parents read these letters aloud at dinner. Then they toss them in the fireplace. The children chant to *La Befana*, the mythical Christmas witch, as their wishes go up the chimney.

When the first star appears in the evening sky on Christmas Eve, every family sets lighted candles in their windows to light the way for the Christ Child. They light candles around their *presepio* and pass the figure of the Baby Jesus from person to person, finally placing it tenderly in the manger. Then they enjoy a lavish meatless supper featuring fish or another type of seafood, vegetables, salads, antipasto, bread, pasta, and sweets. Later that night, everyone goes through the torch-lit streets on their way to Christmas Eve mass.

Christmas Day is reserved for church, family, and feasting. Some Italian children receive gifts from Baby Jesus or from *Babbo Natale*, as Father Christmas is called. Then everyone sits down to a big Christmas dinner. This often includes capon or another roasted meat. *Pannettone*, a yeast cake filled with fruit, and *panforte*, a dense honey cake spiced with cloves and cinnamon, are popular sweets, along with *cassata*, which includes ice cream and fruit.

New Year's Day is when friends get together and visit. It is also the day when Italians exchange gifts with each other. The children have to wait until January 6 to get their gifts from *La Befana*, whose name comes from the Italian word for Epiphany.

January 6 is also called Three Kings Day, because it is the day the Three Kings visited the Christ Child in Bethlehem long ago. The legend says that old *Befana* was too busy cleaning house to help the Wise Men. Now the aged wanderer flies through the air on her broomstick looking for the Christ Child on the eve of Epiphany. Children set out their shoes by the fireplace on that night, hoping for the gifts they asked for during novena. *La Befana* leaves candy and gifts for children who are good.

During the Christmas season, Italian families sing a special song called Shepherds' Carol in honor of the *zampognari*, or real shepherds who came to town at Advent and went from house to house playing bagpipes and singing songs about the birth of Jesus. In some towns, bagpipers dressed as shepherds still play and sing in front of the neighborhoods' *presepios*.

What Child Is This

Words: William Chatterton Dix

Old English

Away in a Manger

Old Lutheran Carol

Slowly, Tenderly

1. A - way in a man-ger, no crib for a bed, The

2. The cattle are lowing, the Baby awakes
But little Lord Jesus, no crying He makes.
I love Thee, Lord Jesus, look down from the sky,
And stay by my cradle till morning is nigh.

3. Be near me, Lord Jesus, I ask Thee to stay
Close by me forever, and love me, I pray.
Bless all the dear children in Thy tender care,
And fit us for Heaven to live with Thee there.

THE STORY OF SILENT NIGHT

Written by Lisa Harkrader
Illustrated by Dick Smolinski

Father Joseph Mohr sat at the old organ. His fingers stretched over the keys, forming the notes of a chord. He took a deep breath and pressed down. Nothing. He lifted his fingers and tried again. Silence echoed through the church.

Father Joseph shook his head. It was no use. The pipes were rusted, the bellows mildewed. The organ had been wheezing and growing quieter for months, and Father Joseph had been hoping it would hold together until the organ builder arrived to repair it in the spring. But now, on December 23, 1818, the organ had finally given out. St. Nicholas Church would have no music for Christmas.

Father Joseph sighed. Maybe a brisk walk would make him feel better. He pulled on his overcoat and stepped out into the night. His white breath puffed out before him. Moonlight sparkled off the snow-crusted trees and houses in the village of Oberndorf. Father Joseph crunched through the snowy streets to the edge of the little Austrian town and climbed the path leading up the mountain.

From high above Oberndorf, Father Joseph watched the Salzach River ripple past St. Nicholas Church. In the spring, when melting snow flowed down the mountains and the river swelled in its banks, water lapped at the foundation of the church. It was moisture from the flooding river that had caused the organ to mildew and rust.

Father Joseph looked out over the Austrian Alps. Stars shone above in the still and silent night.

Silent night? Father Joseph stopped. Of course! "Silent Night!" He had written a poem a few years before, when he had first become a priest, and he had given it that very title. "Silent Night."

Father Joseph scrambled down the mountain. Suddenly he knew how to bring music to the church.

The next morning, Father Joseph set out on another walk. This time he carried his poem. And this time he knew exactly where he was going—to see his friend Franz Gruber, the organist for St. Nicholas, who lived in the next village.

Franz Gruber was surprised to see the priest so far from home on Christmas Eve, and even more surprised when Father Joseph handed him the poem.

That night Father Joseph and Franz Gruber stood at the altar of St. Nicholas Church. Father Joseph held his guitar. He could see members of the congregation giving each other puzzled looks. They had never heard a guitar played in church before, and certainly not during midnight mass on Christmas Eve, the holiest night of the year.

Father Joseph picked out a few notes on the guitar, and he and Franz Gruber began to sing. Their two voices rang out, joined by the church choir on the chorus. Franz Gruber's melody matched the simplicity and honesty of Father Joseph's words.

When the last notes faded into the night, the congregation remained still for a moment, then began to clap their hands. Applause filled the church. The villagers of Oberndorf loved the song! Father Joseph's plan to bring music to St. Nicholas Church had worked.

A few months later, the organ builder arrived in Oberndorf and found the words and music to "Silent Night" lying on the organ. The song enchanted him, and when he left, he took a copy of it with him.

The organ builder gave the song to two families of traveling singers who lived near his home. The traveling singers performed "Silent Night" in concerts all over Europe, and soon the song spread throughout the world.

Today, cathedral choirs and carolers from New York to New Zealand sing the simple song that was first played in a mountain church in Austria on Christmas Eve nearly 200 years ago.

Silent Night

Fr. Joseph Mohr
Franz Gruber

1.Si - lent night, Ho - ly night! All is calm,

all is bright. Round yon Vir - gin Moth - er and

2. Silent night, Holy night!
   Shepherds quake at the sight.
   Glories stream from heaven afar,
   Heav'nly hosts sing Hallelujah,
   Christ the Saviour is born,
   Christ the Saviour is born.

3. Silent night, Holy night!
   Son of God, love's pure light.
   Radiant beams from Thy holy face,
   With the dawn of redeeming grace,
   Jesus Lord at Thy birth,
   Jesus Lord at Thy birth.

CHRISTMAS IN
Germany

Written by Sarah Toast   Illustrated by Sarah Dillard

German families prepare for Christmas throughout cold December. Four Sundays before Christmas, they make an Advent wreath of fir or pine branches with four colored candles. They light a candle on the wreath each Sunday, sing Christmas songs, and eat Christmas cookies. The children count the days until Christmas with an Advent calendar. Each day, they open a little numbered flap on the calendar to see the Christmas picture hidden there.

In the weeks leading up to Christmas, homes are filled with the delightful smells of baking loaves of sweet bread, cakes filled with candied fruits, and spicy cookies called *lebkuchen*.

Bakery windows are filled with displays of lovely marzipan confections in the shape of fruits and animals. Best of all are the famous outdoor Christmas markets. The stalls overflow with all sorts of holiday toys, gifts, decorations, and delicacies.

Many German children write letters to St. Nicholas asking for presents. St. Nicholas Day is December 6. Other German children write their letters to the Christ Child. In some areas, the Christ Child brings gifts to children on St. Nicholas Eve and in other areas on Christmas Eve. He is dressed all in white, with golden wings and a golden crown.

Christmas Eve is the most important time of the Christmas season for families. Some even say it is a magical night when animals can speak. The wonderful tradition of the Christmas tree, which started in Germany, is the heart of the celebration. Grown-ups decorate the evergreen tree with beautiful ornaments of colored glass and carved wood, silver stars, and strings of lights. A golden angel is placed at the very top of the tree.

Under the Christmas tree, the family arranges a manger scene to depict the stable that Jesus was born in. Parents may also pile presents from the Christ Child beneath the Christmas tree's richly decorated boughs. Just after dark, a bell rings, and the excited children run into the room to see the beautiful lighted tree in all its glory. The family members exchange gifts, recite poems, and sing Christmas carols. "Silent Night, Holy Night" is an old German favorite. Then everyone enjoys a Christmas feast of roast goose, turkey, or duck.

In some parts of Germany, families still follow an old tradition. The children leave their shoes outside the front door. These shoes are filled with carrots and hay to feed St. Nicholas' horse as he rides by. If the children were good all year, St. Nicholas leaves apples, nuts, and candy for them.

On Christmas Day the white candle of the Advent wreath is lit. This day is quietly focused on family. They attend church together, and then they eat a delicious Christmas dinner together.

But for the following Twelve Days of Christmas, people in some parts of Germany beat drums to drive off spirits.

On Twelfth Night, or Epiphany, on January 6, boys dress up like the Three Kings who visited Baby Jesus in the manger so long ago. They carry a star on a pole and go through the town singing Christmas carols. Then the family puts away its Christmas decorations for another year, until December comes around again.

THE ELVES AND THE SHOEMAKER

Adapted by Lynne Suesse
Illustrated by Kathleen McCord

There once was a hardworking shoemaker who owned a tiny shop at the edge of town. He was a kind man and always did the best job he could. But times were tough for the shoemaker and his wife. The leather that the shoemaker used to make his shoes was very expensive. After buying the food and firewood that he and his wife needed, he only had enough money to purchase leather for one pair of shoes.

"This will be the finest pair of shoes I make," said the poor shoemaker. "I will start working on it first thing tomorrow morning when the sun is bright and my mind is fresh."

The shoemaker and his wife turned in for the night. As he drifted off to sleep, the shoemaker imagined that the shoes he made were the most wonderful shoes that anyone in the village had ever seen. He saw the bright, shiny buckle that he carefully crafted from silver, and the leather was so finely stitched that the seams were invisible. The tops of the shoes had the most perfect curl that it made the shoemaker giggle!

When the shoemaker awoke the next morning, he could not wait to create the pair of shoes he saw in his dream. The air was still chilly, but the shoemaker felt warm, anticipating the task before him.

As soon as the shoemaker sat down at his workbench, he noticed something quite amazing. The shoes that he pictured in his dreams were sitting right before his eyes right down to the seamless leather, shiny silver buckle, and the perfect little curl!

"Martha! Martha! Come quick!" the shoemaker called to his wife.

When the shoemaker's wife saw the shoes she dropped the plate she had been holding. "Why, those are the most beautiful shoes I've ever seen!" she cried happily. "How did you make them so fast?"

"I didn't. Well, I don't think I did," said the confused shoemaker. "I dreamed about them, but surely I couldn't have made them in my sleep." The shoemaker and his wife stared at the shoes for a little while longer. Then they looked at each other and started laughing. They jumped around the tiny shop and danced for joy!

Just then, the shop door opened. A rich man had been passing through the town and needed a new pair of shoes.

"I heard that you make the finest shoes in all the land," said the stranger.

The shoemaker and his wife quickly stopped dancing and showed the man the mysterious shoes.

"Those are wonderful," said the man. "I must try them on." The rich man slipped them onto his feet and the shoes fit him perfectly!

The stranger was so pleased with the shoes that he bought them immediately. He also insisted on paying the shoemaker two times the price!

"I couldn't have asked for more perfect shoes," said the man. "You must take this money. I wish you both well." With those words, the stranger was out the door.

The shoemaker and his wife began to dance around the shop some more. They could not believe their wonderful fortune.

"We must celebrate," laughed the shoemaker's wife. "I'm going to take some of this money and buy us a ham for supper."

"Don't take too much," said the shoemaker. "I need to buy more leather for my next pair of miraculous shoes."

The shoemaker's wife took only enough money to purchase a fine ham at the butcher. With the rest of the money, the shoemaker was able to buy enough leather for two more pairs of shoes.

After their dinner, the shoemaker was too tired to start working on the new pairs of shoes that night. He cut out the leather, then went to bed, hoping to make a fresh start in the morning.

Once again, the shoemaker had a wonderful dream. This time he saw two pairs of fine shoes. The stitching on each shoe was flawless. The leather had such intricate designs and details! The shoemaker knew that no one in the village had ever seen or owned a pair of such fine shoes. Then the shoemaker awoke again to the bright sunlight streaming through the window.

Again, when the shoemaker sat down at his workbench, the shoes from his dream were sitting before his eyes!

"I can't believe this!" said the shoemaker.

His wife heard the shoemaker's words and came running into the room. "What happened?" she asked breathlessly. Then she saw the two new pairs of shoes and squealed with joy.

The shoemaker and his wife were in the middle of celebrating when once again, the door to the shop opened. This time two customers walked into the shop. They took one look at the two new pairs of shoes and smiled.

"This is exactly what I've been looking for," said the first customer. And when he tried the shoes on, of course, he found that they fit him perfectly!

The second customer was a wealthy woman, who fell in love with the second pair of shoes. "I can't believe what I'm seeing," she said. "This pair will match my new gown that I just had custom made. They're perfect in every way!"

The two customers paid handsomely for each pair of shoes, then quickly left the store. The shoemaker and his wife were left stunned. They could not believe the miracle that took place each night, and they could not believe how quickly the mysterious shoes sold!

Soon the shoemaker's wife gathered some money and ran off to the market to buy a goose for dinner. The shoemaker had enough money left over to purchase leather for four more pairs of shoes!

That evening the shoemaker and his wife enjoyed a feast of roasted goose with all the trimmings. Later that night the shoemaker once again cut out the leather and set it aside to work on in the morning. He went to bed with a full belly and a happy heart. As he dreamed that night, he saw the leather that he bought forming itself into beautiful shoes, as if by magic. As he dreamed some more, he could see that the leather was actually being worked by tiny hands, not much bigger than the head of a hat pin.

When the shoemaker awoke the next morning, he called to his wife. "Have you seen them?" he asked her excitedly. "Have you seen the shoes? Are they there?"

The shoemaker and his wife quickly ran to the workbench. Sure enough, four pairs of elegant shoes sat before them. They were exactly as the shoemaker had seen them in his dream.

"This is amazing," said the shoemaker's wife. "How is this happening?"

The shoemaker shook his head. "I can't be sure, but in my dream I saw tiny hands working the leather and stitching the stitches."

As the shoemaker shrugged his shoulders, four customers hurried into the shop. Like the customers before, they were delighted with what they saw. The new shoes were gone in a blink of an eye, and the shoemaker and his wife had more money than they had ever dreamed.

"I do believe our money troubles are over, Martha," said the shoemaker, happily. "But we must not let all this success go to our heads."

For several weeks, the mysterious activities continued in the middle of the night. Each morning beautiful and wonderful shoes were waiting for the shoemaker and his wife. Now they were no longer poor. In fact, they were quite well-off.

It was almost Christmas Day. The shoemaker and his wife gave thanks for all their good fortune. But they did not know who to thank for making such fabulous shoes.

"Martha, I think it's about time we find out who is doing this tremendous favor for us," said the shoemaker.

"I quite agree! We need to make sure the mysterious stranger has a wonderful Christmas like ours," said the shoemaker's wife.

The shoemaker and his wife agreed that they would stay awake that night to see the secret stranger arrive. They hid behind a bookcase with just a candle for light.

As the clock struck midnight, the shoemaker and his wife were amazed at what they saw. It was not one mysterious stranger, but two tiny elves who came prancing in through the window! The elves were wearing barely a stitch of clothing and old worn-out rags on their feet instead of shoes. The little elves seemed happy, though, as their tiny feet crossed the room. They immediately started working on the leather left on top of the workbench—their tiny hands sewing each stitch perfectly.

"That's why I saw tiny hands in my dreams!" whispered the shoemaker excitedly. "Look at how swiftly they work! It is a miracle indeed!"

"They are the sweetest-looking creatures I have ever seen," said the shoemaker's wife. "They are just like tiny children, small enough to fit in my pocket!"

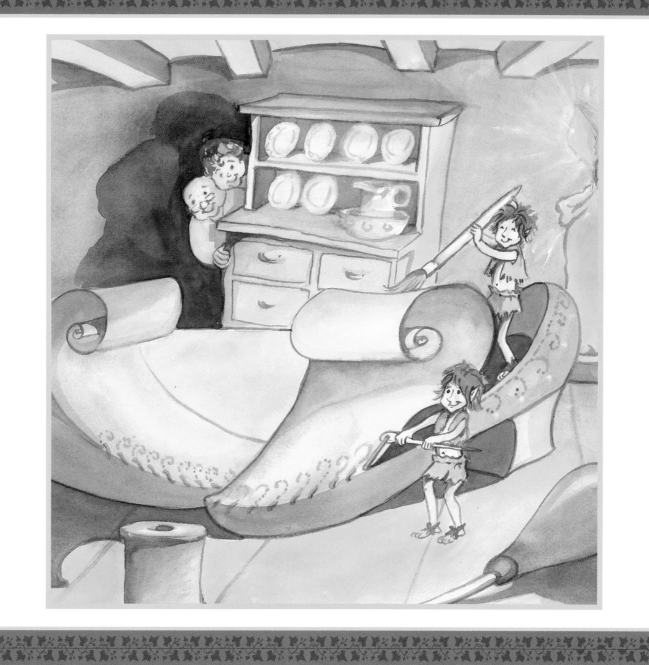

When the two elves had finished their work, they quickly and quietly left the way they came. The shoemaker and his wife looked at each other in disbelief. The sun was coming up, so the shoemaker's wife began breakfast while the shoemaker took the new shoes and opened shop for the day.

Later that day, the shoemaker's wife said, "I've been thinking that it is a shame that those dear little elves work so hard to make us these wonderful shoes and they don't even have any proper shoes or clothing."

"I've been thinking the same thing," replied the shoemaker. "I think I'll take some of these scraps of leather and make the elves some brand-new shoes."

"And I'll make them each a fine suit of clothing," said the shoemaker's wife.

The shoemaker and his wife worked all evening to make the tiny elves a new set of clothes. By the time night fell, each elf had a tiny pair of pants, a shirt, a hat, and an overcoat. The shoemaker had even created a fine pair of leather shoes, just the right size for each of their elfin feet.

"Oh, these clothes are just perfect for our little helpers!" cried the shoemaker's wife. "I can't wait to see what happens when they see these outfits!"

"I do believe that these clothes will suit our friends nicely," said the shoemaker, as he grinned proudly.

As the hour grew late, the shoemaker and his wife waited behind the bookcase for the elves to arrive. Their hearts were beating quickly with anticipation. They could not wait to see the look on the elves' faces when they saw their brand-new outfits.

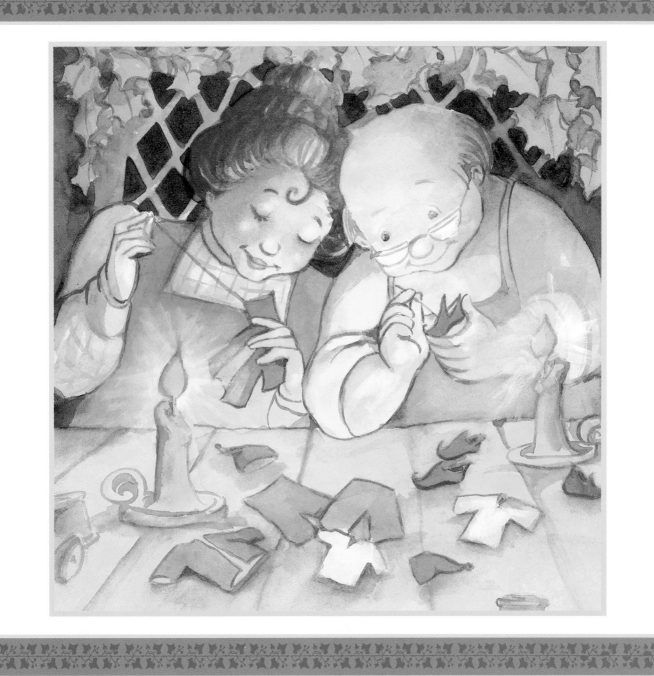

Just then the clock struck midnight. The shoemaker and his wife held their breath as they watched the workbench closely. Just like the night before, the two tiny elves pranced through the window, shivering from the cold night air. As soon as they got to the workbench, they saw the fine sets of clothing.

"Hooray!" the elves cried, as they touched each piece of clothing. They quickly dressed in their new clothes. The elves were so happy they began to dance and sing.

The shoemaker and his wife were so delighted to see the tiny elves celebrating. After all, the elves had helped them when they really needed it most.

After lots of joyful dancing around the workbench, the elves suddenly turned and left the shoemaker's shop. Their tiny giggles could be heard in the crisp night air as they disappeared through the window.

The shoemaker and his wife never saw the elves again, but they had made so much money from selling the elves' shoes, that the shoemaker was able to buy enough fine leather to keep the shop going. The shoemaker and his wife were never poor again. They had a wonderful Christmas season and were able to share their Christmas joy with the rest of the town.

The shoemaker and his wife never forgot those magical elves and every now and then they thought they heard the giggling of the little elves.

"Merry Christmas, little friends," said the shoemaker into the night air. He drifted off to sleep and dreamed a wonderful dream of the tiny elves making someone else's Christmas dreams come true.

Christmas Greeting
From a Fairy to a Child

Written by Lewis Carroll
Illustrated by Robin Bell Corfield

Lady, dear, if Fairies may
   For a moment lay aside
Cunning tricks and elfish play,
   'Tis at happy Christmas-tide.

We have heard the children say,
   Gentle children, whom we love,
Long ago on Christmas Day,
   Came a message from above.

Still as Christmas-tide comes round,
    They remember it again.
Echo still the joyful sounds
    "Peace on earth, good-will to men!"

Yet the hearts must childlike be
    Where such heavenly guests abide;
Unto children, in their glee,
    All the year is Christmas-tide!

Thus, forgetting tricks and play
    For a moment, Lady dear,
We would wish you, if we may,
    Merry Christmas, glad New Year!

CHRISTMAS IN

France

Written by Sarah Toast

Illustrated by Marty Noble

Christmas in France is a family holiday. The celebrations begin on December 5, which is St. Nicholas Eve. It is a day for gift-giving between friends and relatives. On that cold night, children leave their shoes by the hearth so *Père Noël*, or Father Christmas, will fill them with gifts.

Christmas Eve is the most special time in the French celebration of Christmas. Church bells ring and voices sing French carols, called *noëls*.

The family fasts all day, then everyone but the youngest children goes to midnight mass. The churches and cathedrals are beautifully lit, and most display a lovely antique *crèche*. Afterward, the family returns home to a nighttime feast that is called *le réveillon*. The menu is different in the various regions of France. In Paris, it might be oysters and paté, while in Brittany, the traditional midnight supper is buckwheat cakes and sour cream.

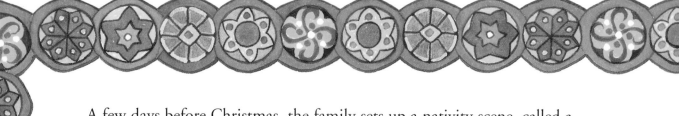

A few days before Christmas, the family sets up a nativity scene, called a *crèche*, on a little platform in a corner of the living room. Some families also decorate a Christmas tree with colorful stars, lights, and tinsel, but the *crèche* is much more important. The tradition in Provence, in the south of France, is to include, along with the Holy Family, the Three Kings, the shepherds, and the animals, delightful little figures from village life dressed in old-fashioned costumes. These figures might include a village mayor, a peasant, a gypsy, a drummer boy, and other colorful characters. Another tradition in Provence is for people to dress as shepherds and take part in a procession that circles the local church.

To complete the elaborate *crèche* in their home, children bring moss, stones, and evergreen branches for the finishing touches. When the candles are lit, the *crèche* becomes the centerpiece of the Christmas celebration. The children gather around it to sing carols every night until Epiphany, on January 6.

Christmas plays and puppet shows are popular entertainments at Christmas, especially in Paris and Lyons. The shop windows of large department stores have wonderful displays of animated figures that families like to visit.

If any children did not leave their shoes out to be filled with gifts by *Père Noël* on St. Nicholas Eve, they leave them out on Christmas Eve to be filled by *Père Noël* or the Baby Jesus. Before going to bed, some families leave food and a candle burning, in case Mary passes by with the Christ Child. In homes that have a Christmas tree, *Père Noël* hangs little toys, candies, and fruits on the tree's branches for the sleeping children.

On Christmas Day, the family goes to church again and then enjoys another abundant feast of wonderful dishes, ending with the traditional *bûche de Noël*, a rich buttercream-filled cake shaped and frosted to look like a Yule log.

On New Year's, grown-ups visit their friends to exchange gifts with them and enjoy yet more feasting at the New Year's *réveillon*. The family gathers together again for a final feast on Epiphany on January 6. They eat a special flat pastry, a *galette*, that has a tiny old-fashioned shoe, a very little china doll, or a bean baked in it. Whoever finds the prize in their serving gets to be King or Queen for the day. As church bells ring, the celebration of the Christmas season comes to an end.

The First Noel

Old English

2. They looked up and saw a star
   Shining in the East beyond them far,
   And to the earth it gave great light,
   And so it continued both day and night.
   Noel, etc.

3. This star drew nigh to the northwest,
   O'er Bethlehem it took its rest.
   And there it did both stop and stay
   Right over the place where Jesus lay.
   Noel, etc.

CHRISTMAS IN

Spain

Written by Sarah Toast

Illustrated by Carolyn Croll

The Christmas season begins in Spain on December 8, with a weeklong observance of the Feast of the Immaculate Conception. Spanish families may travel to Seville, in the southwest, where the warm weather encourages flowers to bloom in December. In Seville's great cathedral, they watch ten costumed boys perform an ancient dance called *Los Seises* to honor the Virgin Mary, the patron saint of Spain. In northern Spain, families decorate their balconies with colorful carpets, flags, and flowers. They burn candles all night in the windows.

Evergreens decorate the churches and outdoor markets throughout the Christmas season. Tambourines, gourd rattles, castanets, and miniature guitars are offered for sale to enliven the singing and dancing in the streets. Children go from house to house reciting verses or singing carols for sweets, toys, or small instruments.

Life-size nativity scenes called *nacimientos* are set up in public places, and every family has a small *nacimiento* in the best room in the house. In some villages, families send their sons to bring in a Yule log. As the boys tug the log home, they stop at homes along the way for chocolates and nuts.

Christmas Eve is *La Noche Buena*, the Blessed Night. When the first star shines in the evening sky, people light bonfires, called *luminarias*, in public squares and outside church walls. Traditional plays called *Las Pastores* depict the shepherds' adoration of the Christ Child in Bethlehem.

At home, each family places a burning candle above the door and lights candles around the *nacimiento*. People fast all day and then go as a family to midnight mass. Then they return home to enjoy a feast of almond soup, roasted meat, baked red cabbage, and sweet potato or pumpkin.

Christmas Day is set aside for family reunions, when relatives get together for more feasting. The children sing and dance around the *nacimiento*. Family members exchange gifts, and friends and neighbors exchange holiday sweets.

Some families add to the fun with the traditional Urn of Fate. Names are written on cards and placed in a bowl. Then two names are drawn at a time. Those two people will be friendly to each other throughout the coming year.

Children believe that on Epiphany Eve, January 5, the Three Kings travel through Spain on their way to Bethlehem. That night children set out their shoes filled with straw for the Three Kings' camels. The Kings, passing in the night, fill the shoes with gifts. The next day, families enjoy a feast of almond soup, turkey, and roasted chestnuts. Sweets include a special nougat candy called *turrón* and Kings' cake. A small prize baked in the cake brings luck to the person who finds it.

In some villages on Epiphany, January 6, children march out to the city gates carrying special cakes for the Three Kings and other foods for their servants and camels. They are hoping to meet the Three Kings on their way to the Holy Land. Always disappointed in their hopes, the children eat the good things they have brought with them. Then they are directed by their parents to the *nacimiento* in the village church. There they find the Three Kings presenting gifts to the Christ Child in a manger.

The Christmas season ends at Epiphany with the "Cavalcade of the Kings," a wonderful parade of the Three Kings and live animals.

We Three Kings

John H. Hopkins

THE GIFT OF THE MAGI

Written by O. Henry
Illustrated by Dick Smolinski

One dollar and eighty-seven cents. That was all. And sixty-seven cents of it was in pennies. Pennies saved one, two, and three at a time by negotiating with the grocer and the vegetable man and the butcher until one's cheeks burned with embarrassment. Three times Della counted it. One dollar and eighty-seven cents. And the next day would be Christmas.

There was clearly nothing to do but flop down on the shabby little couch and howl. So Della did it. She was beginning to believe that life was made up of sobs, sniffles, and smiles, with sniffles predominating.

While the mistress of the home is gradually subsiding from the first stage to the second, take a look at the home. A furnished flat at $8 per week.

In the vestibule below was a letter-box into which no letter would go, and an electric doorbell from which no mortal finger could coax a ring. Also there was a card bearing the name "Mr. James Dillingham Young."

The "Dillingham" had been flung to the breeze during a former period of prosperity when its possessor was being paid $30 per week. Now, when the income was shrunk to $20, though, they were thinking seriously of contracting to a modest and unassuming "D." But whenever Mr. James Dillingham Young came home and reached his flat above he was called "Jim" and greatly hugged by Mrs. James Dillingham Young, already introduced to you as Della. Which is all very good.

Della finished her cry and attended to her cheeks with the powder rag. She stood by the window and looked out dully at a gray cat walking a gray fence in a gray backyard. Tomorrow would be Christmas Day, and she had only $1.87 with which to buy Jim a present. She had been saving every penny she could for months, with this result. Twenty dollars a week does not go far. Expenses had been greater than she had calculated. Only $1.87 to buy a present for Jim. Many a happy hour she had spent planning for something nice for him, something fine and rare and sterling, something just a little bit near to being worthy of the honor of being owned by Jim.

There was a pier-glass between the windows of the room. Perhaps you have seen a pier-glass in an $8 flat. A very thin and very agile person may, by observing his reflection in a rapid sequence of mirrored strips, obtain a fairly accurate conception of his looks. Della, being slender, had mastered the art.

Suddenly she whirled from the window and stood before the glass. Her eyes were shining brilliantly, but her face had lost its color within twenty seconds. Rapidly she pulled down her hair and let it fall to its full length.

Now, there were two possessions of the James Dillingham Youngs in which they both took a mighty pride. One was Jim's gold watch that had been his father's and his grandfather's. The other was Della's hair. Had the queen of Sheba lived in the flat across the air shaft, Della would have let her hair hang out the window to dry just to depreciate Her Majesty's jewels and gifts. Had King Solomon been the janitor, with all his treasures piled up in the basement, Jim would have pulled out his watch every time he passed, just to see him pluck at his beard from envy.

So now Della's beautiful hair fell about her, rippling and shining like a cascade of brown waters. It reached below her waist and made itself almost a garment for her. And then she did it up again nervously and quickly.

On went her old brown jacket; on went her old brown hat. With a whirl of skirts and with the brilliant sparkle still in her eyes, she fluttered out the door and down the stairs to the street.

Where she stopped the sign read: "Madame Sofronie. Hair Goods of All Kinds." One flight up Della ran, and collected herself, panting. Madame Sofronie was large, chilly, and too white. She hardly looked the "Sofronie."

"Will you buy my hair?" asked Della.

"I buy hair," said Madame. "Take yer hat off and let's have a sight at the looks of it."

Down rippled the brown cascade.

"Twenty dollars," said Madame, lifting the mass with a practiced hand.

"Give it to me quick," said Della.

The next two hours tripped by on rosy wings. Della was ransacking the stores for Jim's present.

She found it at last. It surely had been made for Jim and no one else. There was no other like it in any of the stores, and she had turned all of them inside out. It was a platinum fob chain, simple and chaste in design, properly proclaiming its value by substance alone.

As soon as she saw it she knew that it must be Jim's. It was like him. Quietness and value, the description applied to both. Twenty-one dollars they took from her for it, and she hurried home with the eighty-seven cents. With that chain on his watch Jim might be properly anxious about the time in any company. Grand as the watch was, he sometimes looked at it on the sly on account of the old leather strap that he used in place of a chain.

When Della reached home her intoxication gave way a little to prudence and reason. She got out her curling irons and lighted the gas and went to work repairing the ravages made by generosity added to love.

Within forty minutes her head was covered with tiny, close-lying curls that made her look wonderfully like a truant schoolboy. She looked at her reflection in the mirror long, carefully, and critically.

"If Jim doesn't kill me," she said to herself, "before he takes a second look at me, he'll say I look like a Coney Island chorus girl. But what could I do? Oh! what could I do with a dollar and eighty-seven cents?"

At seven o'clock the coffee was made and the frying pan was sitting on the back of the stove. It was hot and ready to cook the pork chops that Della had bought the night before.

Jim was never late. Della doubled the fob chain in her hand and sat on the corner of the table near the door that he always entered. She waited impatiently for him to come home.

Then Della heard his step on the stairs way down on the first flight. Quickly, she stood up and fixed her hair one last time. Then she turned white for just a moment. Della had a habit of saying little silent prayers about the simplest everyday things, and now she whispered, "Please God, make him think I am still pretty. Make him love me just the same."

The door opened and Jim stepped in and closed it. He looked thin and very serious. Poor fellow, he was only twenty-two and already burdened with a family! He needed a new overcoat and he was without gloves.

"Hello, dear," Jim said. Then he looked up at Della. Jim stopped inside the door, as immovable as a setter at the scent of quail. His eyes were fixed upon Della as she stood in front of the pier-glass.

Della tried to smile, until she looked into his eyes. There was an expression in them that she could not read, and it terrified her. It was not anger, nor surprise, nor disapproval, nor horror, nor any of the sentiments that she had been prepared for. He simply stared at her fixedly with that peculiar expression on his face.

Della finally moved and went for him. "Jim, darling," she cried, "please don't look at me that way. I had my hair cut off and sold because I could not have lived through Christmas without giving you a real present. And I certainly didn't have enough money saved."

Della held Jim's hands and looked into his eyes. "It will grow out again," she said. "You won't mind, will you? I just had to do it. My hair grows awfully fast. Please say 'Merry Christmas!' Jim, and let's be happy. You don't know what a beautiful, nice gift I have for you."

"You've cut off your hair?" asked Jim, as if he had not arrived at that patent fact yet even after the hardest mental labor.

Della held his hand tighter still, warming it with her own. "Cut it off and sold it," said Della. "Don't you like me just as well, anyhow? I'm me without my hair. Don't you think so?"

Jim looked about the room curiously. "You say your hair is gone?" he said, with an air almost of idiocy.

"You needn't look for it," said Della. "It's sold, I tell you, sold and gone, too. It's Christmas Eve, boy. Be good to me, for it went for you. Maybe the hairs of my head were numbered," she went on with sudden serious sweetness, "but nobody could ever count my love for you."

Della waited for Jim to speak then. He took off his coat without speaking and then turned back to Della.

Out of his trance Jim seemed quickly to wake. He grabbed Della in his arms.

For ten seconds let us regard with discreet scrutiny some inconsequential object in the other direction. Eight dollars a week or a million a year, what is the difference? A mathematician would give you the wrong answer. The Magi brought valuable gifts, but that was not among them. This dark assertion will be illuminated later on.

Jim drew a package from his overcoat pocket and threw it upon the table. "Do not make a mistake, Dell, about me," he said. "I don't think there is anything in the way of a haircut or a shave or a shampoo that could make me like my girl any less. But if you will unwrap that small package you may see why you had me going a while at first."

White, nimble fingers tore at the string and paper. Della let out an ecstatic scream of joy. Then her voice turned to hysterical tears and wails as she examined the contents of the box.

For there lay "the combs," the set of combs, side and back, that Della had worshiped long in a Broadway window. Beautiful combs, pure tortoise shell, with jeweled rims, just the shade to wear in the beautiful vanished hair. They were very expensive combs, she knew, and her heart had simply craved and yearned over them without the least hope of possession. And now, they were hers, but the tresses that should have adorned the coveted adornments were gone.

Jim summoned up all of his comforting powers and said, "I can take the combs back and get the money."

But she hugged them to her bosom, and at length she was able to look up with dim eyes and a smile and say, "My hair grows so fast, Jim!"

And then Della leaped up like a little singed cat and cried, "Oh, oh!" She ran to the table and opened the box for Jim.

Jim had not yet seen his beautiful present. She held it out to him eagerly upon her open palm. The dull precious metal seemed to flash with a reflection of her bright and ardent spirit.

"Isn't it a dandy, Jim?" Della asked. "I hunted all over town to find it. You'll have to look at the time a hundred times a day now. Give me your watch. I want to see how it looks on it."

Instead of obeying, Jim tumbled down on the couch and put his hands under the back of his head and smiled.

"Dell," said Jim, "let's put our Christmas presents away and keep them a while. They're too nice to use just yet. I sold the watch to get the money to buy your combs. And now suppose we get dinner ready."

The Magi, as you know, were wise men who brought gifts to the Babe in the manger. They invented the art of giving Christmas presents. And here I have lamely related to you the uneventful chronicle of two foolish children in a flat who most unwisely sacrificed for each other the greatest treasures of their house. But in a last word to the wise of these days let it be said that of all who give gifts these two were the wisest. Of all who give and receive gifts, they are wisest. They are the Magi.

What Can I Give Him

Written by Christina Rossetti
Illustrated by John Lund

What can I give Him, poor as I am?

If I were a shepherd, I would bring a lamb.

If I were a Wise Man, I would do my part,

Yet what can I give Him, give my heart.

THE LEGEND OF THE POINSETTIA

Written by Stephanie Herbek
Illustrated by Carolyn Croll

Maria and Pablo lived in a tiny village in Mexico. Because Christmastime at their house did not include many gifts, Maria and Pablo looked forward to the Christmas festivities at the village church with great joy and anticipation. To honor the birth of Christ, the church displayed a beautiful manger that drew crowds of admirers. Villagers walked miles to admire the manger, bringing lovely, expensive gifts for the Baby Jesus. As Maria and Pablo watched the villagers place their gifts in the soft hay around the manger, they felt sad. They had no money to buy gifts for their family and no money to buy a gift for the Baby Jesus.

One Christmas Eve, Maria and Pablo walked to the church for that evening's services, wishing desperately that they had a gift to bring. Just then, a soft glowing light shone through the darkness, and the shadowy outline of an angel appeared above them.

Maria and Pablo were afraid, but the angel comforted them, instructing them to pick some of the short green weeds that were growing by the road. They should bring the plants to the church, the angel explained, and place them near the manger as their gift to the Baby Jesus. Then just as quickly as she had appeared, the angel was gone, leaving Maria and Pablo on the road looking up into the dark sky. Confused but excited, the children filled their arms with large bunches of the green weeds and hurried to the church.

When the children entered the church, many of the villagers turned to stare. As Maria and Pablo began placing the weeds around the manger, some of the villagers laughed at them. "Why are those children putting weeds by the manger?" they asked each other. Maria and Pablo began to feel embarrassed and ashamed of their gift to the Baby Jesus, but they stood bravely near the manger, placing the plants on the soft hay, as the angel had instructed.

Suddenly, the dull green leaves on the tops of the plants began to turn a beautiful shade of red, surrounding the Baby with beautiful blooms. The laughing villagers became silent as they watched the green plants transform into the lovely star-shaped crimson flowers we call poinsettias. As they watched the weeds bloom before their eyes, Maria and Pablo knew they had no reason to be ashamed anymore. They had given the Baby Jesus the only gift they could—and it was the most beautiful gift of all.

Today, poinsettias are a traditional symbol of Christmas, thanks to young Maria and Pablo and their special gifts to the Baby Jesus.

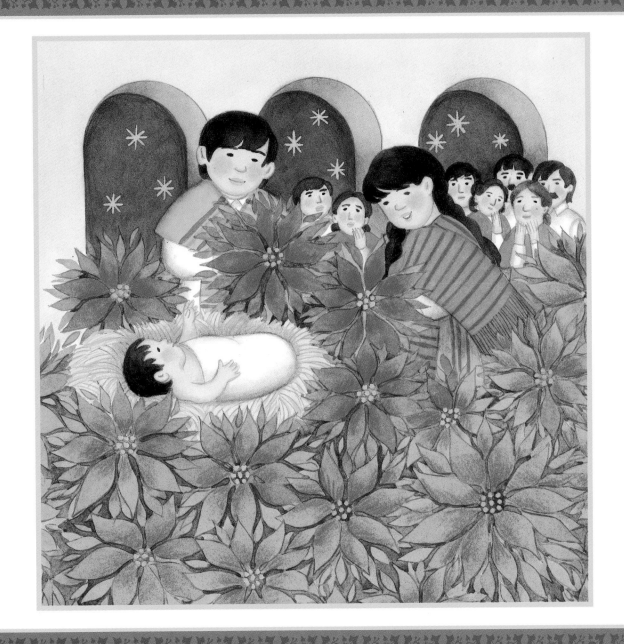

CHRISTMAS IN

Mexico

Written by Sarah Toast

Illustrated by Carolyn Croll

The weather is warm and mild in Mexico during the Christmas season. Families shop for gifts, ornaments, and good things to eat in the market stalls called *puestos*. They decorate their homes with lilies and evergreens. Family members cut intricate designs in brown paper bags to make lanterns called *farolitos*. They place a candle inside and then set the *farolitos* along sidewalks, on windowsills, and on rooftops and outdoor walls to illuminate the community with the spirit of Christmas.

The Mexican celebration of Christmas is called *las posadas* and begins on December 16. The ninth evening of *las posadas* is *Buena Noche*, Christmas Eve. The children lead a procession to the church and place a figure of the Christ Child in the *nacimiento* or nativity scene there. Then everyone attends midnight mass.

186

After mass, the church bells ring out and fireworks light up the skies. Many Mexican children receive gifts from Santa Claus on this night. The children help to set up the family's *nacimiento* in the best room in the house. The scene includes a little hillside, the stable, and painted clay figures of the Holy Family, shepherds, the Three Kings, and animals. The children bring moss, rocks, and flowers to complete the scene.

Families begin the nine-day observance of *las posadas* by reenacting the Holy Family's nine-day journey to Bethlehem and their search for shelter in a *posada*, or inn. In some parts of Mexico, for the first eight evenings of *las posadas* two costumed children carry small statues of Mary and Joseph as they lead a candlelight procession of friends and neighbors from house to house. They sing a song asking for shelter for the weary travelers. When at last they find a family that will give shelter, the children say a prayer of thanks and place the figures of Mary and Joseph in the family's *nacimiento*. Then everyone enjoys a feast at the home of one of the participants.

For the children, the *piñata* party on the first eight evenings is the best part of *las posadas*. The *piñata* is a large clay or papier-mâché figure shaped like a star, an animal, or some other object and covered with colorful paper streamers. The *piñata* is filled with candy or small gifts and hung from the ceiling. The blindfolded children are spun around and given a big stick.

They take turns trying to break open the *piñata* with the stick while the *piñata* is raised and lowered. Everybody scrambles for the gifts and treats when the *piñata* shatters and spills its treasure.

Christmas Day is a time for church and family. After church services, Christmas dinner begins with oxtail soup with beans and hot chili, followed by roasted turkey and a special salad of fresh fruits and vegetables.

Many children receive gifts on the eve of Twelfth Night, January 5, from the *Reyes Magos,* the Three Kings who pass through on their way to Bethlehem. Children leave their shoes on the windowsill and find them filled with gifts the next morning. At a special Twelfth Night supper on January 6, families and friends enjoy hot chocolate flavored with vanilla and cinnamon, and a ring-shaped cake. Whoever gets the slice of cake containing a tiny figure of a baby will give a tamale party on February 2, Candlemas Day. The whole family helps to prepare the tamales, which are a meat or chicken filling wrapped in corn dough. The tamale is then wrapped in corn husks and steamed. A religious service held on Candlemas marks the end of the Christmas season in Mexico.

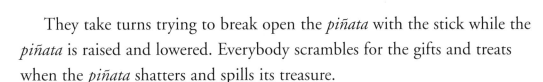

The Twelve Days of Christmas

Traditional

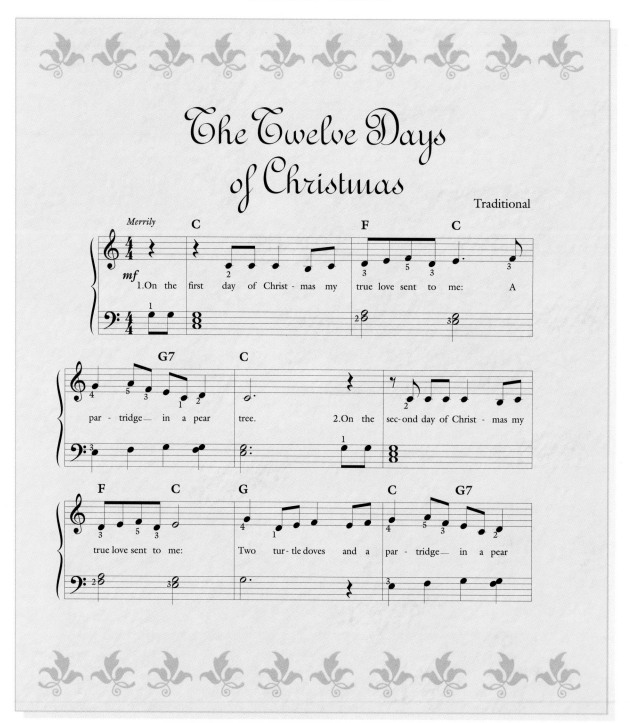

IS THERE A SANTA CLAUS

Written by Francis P. Church

Illustrated by Mike Jaroszko

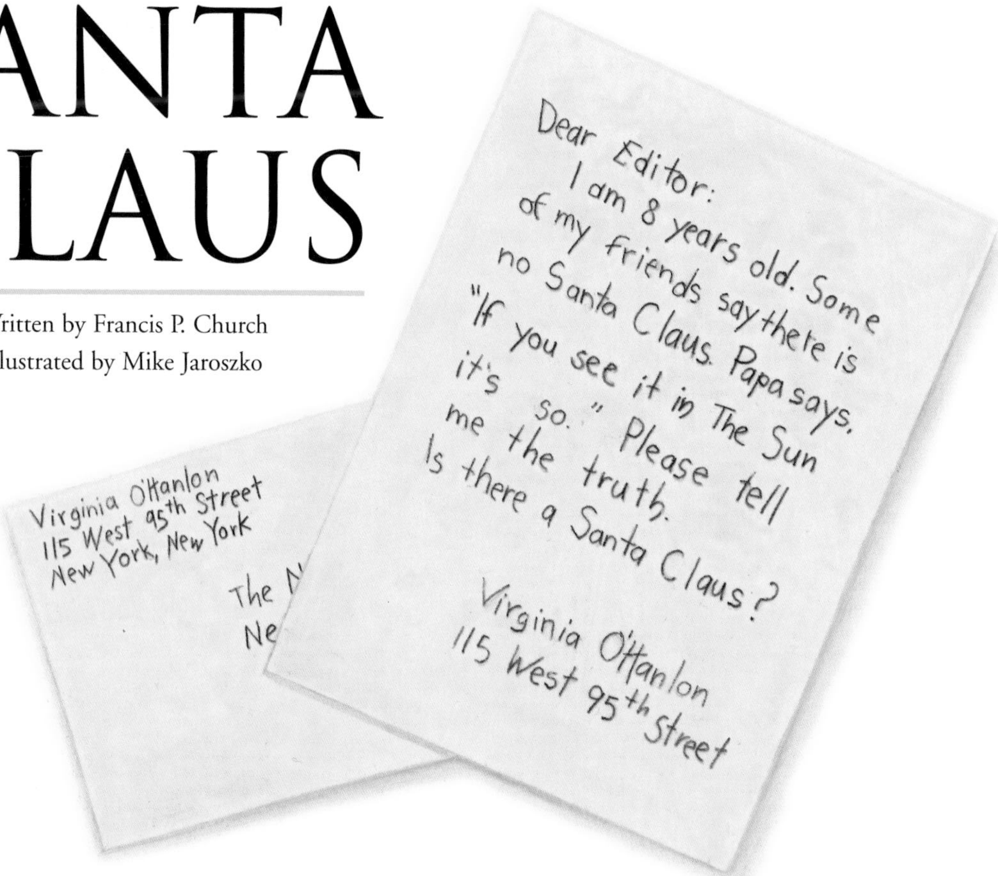

Dear Editor:
I am 8 years old. Some of my friends say there is no Santa Claus. Papa says, "If you see it in The Sun it's so." Please tell me the truth. Is there a Santa Claus?

Virginia O'Hanlon
115 West 95th Street

Virginia O'Hanlon
115 West 95th Street
New York, New York

The N
Ne

Yes, Virginia, there is a Santa Claus

By Francis P. Church
NEW YORK SUN EDITOR

Virginia, your little friends are wrong. They have been affected by the skepticism of a skeptical age. They do not believe except they see. They think that nothing can be which is not comprehensible by their little minds. All minds, Virginia, whether they be men's or children's, are little. In this great universe of ours man is a mere insect, an ant, in his intellect, as compared with the boundless world about him, as measured by the intelligence capable of grasping the whole of truth and knowledge.

Yes, Virginia, there is a Santa Claus. He exists as certainly as love and generosity and devotion exist, and you know that they abound and give to your life at its highest beauty and joy. Alas! How dreary would be the world if there were no Santa Claus! It would be as dreary as if there were no Virginias. There would be no childlike faith then, no poetry, no romance to make tolerable this existence. We should have no enjoyment, except in sense and sight. The eternal light with which childhood fills the world would be extinguished.

Not believe in Santa Claus! You might as well not believe in fairies! You might get your papa to hire men to watch in all the chimneys on Christmas Eve to catch Santa Claus, but even if they did not see Santa Claus coming down, what would that prove?

Nobody sees Santa Claus, but that is no sign that there is no Santa Claus. The most real things in the world are those that neither children nor men can see.

Did you ever see fairies dancing on the lawn? Of course not, but that's no proof that they are not there. Nobody can conceive or imagine all the wonders there are unseen and unseeable in the world.

You tear apart the baby's rattle and see what makes the noise inside, but there is a veil covering the unseen world which not the strongest man, not even the united strength of all the strongest men that ever lived, could tear apart. Only faith, fancy, poetry, love, romance, can push aside that curtain and view and picture the supernal beauty and glory beyond. Is it all real? Ah, Virginia, in all this world there is nothing else real and abiding.

No Santa Claus! Thank God, he lives, and he lives forever. A thousand years from now, Virginia, nay, ten times ten thousand years from now, he will continue to make glad the heart of childhood.

The New York Sun,
September 21, 1897

Jolly Old St. Nicholas

American

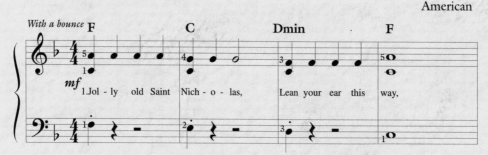

With a bounce

1.Jol - ly old Saint Nich - o - las, Lean your ear this way,

2. When the clock is striking twelve,
   When I'm fast asleep,
   Down the chimney broad and black,
   With your pack you'll creep.

   All the stockings you will find
   Hanging in a row.
   Mine will be the shortest one,
   You'll be sure to know.

CHRISTMAS IN
 China

Written by Sarah Toast   Illustrated by Robin Bell Corfield

The small number of Christians in China call Christmas *Sheng Dan Jieh*, which means Holy Birth Festival. They decorate their homes with evergreens, posters, and bright paper chains. The family puts up a Christmas tree, called "tree of light," and decorates it with beautiful lanterns, flowers, and red paper chains that symbolize happiness. They cut out red pagodas to paste on the windows, and they light their houses with paper lanterns, too.

Many Chinese enjoy the fun and color that Christmas brings to the drab winter season. Big cities like Beijing, Shanghai, and Hong Kong are gaily decorated at Christmas. Many people give parties on Christmas Eve, and some people enjoy a big Christmas dinner at a restaurant. Shops sell plastic trees and Christmas decorations for everyone to enjoy, and Santa Claus is a popular good-luck figure.

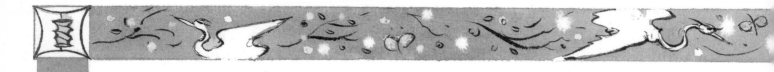

The Christmas season is ushered in with fireworks. Jugglers and acrobats entertain, and people enjoy the merriment and feasting. In Hong Kong, which recently was restored to Chinese rule, Christmas Day is just one of seventeen public holidays. At this time of year, people in Hong Kong also celebrate *Ta Chiu*, a festival of peace and renewal, by making offerings to saints and reading the names of everyone who lives in the area.

On Christmas Eve, Christian children in China hang up their muslin stockings that are specially made so *Dun Che Lao Ren*, or "Christmas Old Man," can fill them with wonderful gifts. Santa Claus may also be called *Lan Khoong-Khoong*, "Nice Old Father."

The Chinese lunar New Year, or Spring Festival, begins in late January or early February. The celebration lasts for three days. While not part of Christmas, the New Year is the most important celebration of the year for the Chinese people. People travel long distances to be with their families. They decorate their homes with brightly colored banners. These banners carry messages of good wishes for the coming year.

Many people exchange gifts at the New Year. Following tradition, very expensive, special presents are given only to close family members. Token gifts are given to friends and distant relations. Children especially enjoy their gifts of new shoes and hats.

People put on new clothes for the New Year celebration. They prepare many special holiday dishes, and families come together at one house to enjoy them. The younger sons of the household serve dinner to the head of the household.

For the first celebration, on New Year's Day, people offer rice, vegetables, tea, and wine to heaven and earth. They burn incense and candles to pay tribute to their ancestors and to all living members of the family.

Chinese families turn out to watch the spectacular New Year's fireworks displays and the exciting lion dance. Several performers dance inside an enormous costume. They make the "lion" walk, slither, glide, leap, and crouch along the street as it leads a colorful procession.

The greatest spectacle takes place at the Feast of the Lanterns, when everyone lights at least one lantern for the occasion. Other special events of the New Year include the Festival of the Dragons and the Fisherman's Festival.

Throughout the three days of New Year's celebrations, everyone speaks only cheerful words to each other so they will have good luck in the coming year.

THE TRUE STORY OF
SANTA CLAUS

Written by Brian Conway
Illustrated by Mike Jaroszko

Santa Claus was not always a jolly old fellow. He did not always have long white whiskers, and he did not always wear a big red suit.

Long before he lived in the North Pole, and long before his yearly Christmas visits brought joy to all the children of the world, Santa Claus was a child himself. He was once just an ordinary baby boy named Nicholas.

The baby boy was just like any other, but his parents hoped for great things from their only son. They named him Nicholas, which means "hero of the people."

Even at a young age, Nicholas was a kind and generous boy. He often helped the people in his village. He shared his meals with those who had nothing to eat, he was always the first to lend a helping hand, and he brought joy to young and old alike. There was no better friend to have than young Nicholas.

At a very young age, Nicholas joined the church. It was his duty to help people. Nicholas gave special attention to the children of his village, and they were very fond of Nicholas for his playful and joyful manner.

Nicholas became well-known throughout the land as a kind and wise young man. He was soon named a bishop of the church. Because Nicholas was still so young, people called him the "Boy Bishop."

Nicholas wore a long red robe with a red hat, and he traveled on horseback. At every village, happy children would spot his bright robe from a distance and gather in the road to greet him.

In one village, Bishop Nicholas heard the sorrowful tale of a poor old man and his three young daughters. It seemed the man could no longer feed his daughters, and he feared he would have to send them away from him. Nicholas knew he could help this family.

That night, while the whole village slept, Nicholas crept up to the hut where the three sisters lived. He climbed up to the rooftop to find the chimney. There Nicholas dropped three bags of gold, one by one, down through the chimney stack.

Earlier that day, the three sisters had hung their newly washed stockings by the fireplace to dry. Each small bag of gold that Nicholas dropped fell into one of the stockings below.

The next morning, the girls were overjoyed to find gold coins in their stockings. "Father!" they called, running to wake him. "We have received a magical gift!"

As the story of these three sisters spread from village to village, other people began to hang their stockings by the fire, hoping to find a secret gift when they awoke the next morning.

Though this was Bishop Nicholas' most famous gift, it was not his first good deed. And it would certainly not be his last.

Bishop Nicholas enjoyed surprising people. He began to deliver his secret gifts of hope and joy only at night, while his friends were asleep.

For all of his good deeds, Bishop Nicholas was named a saint. He is honored as the saint who looks after all children.

Like other saints, St. Nicholas was given a name day. One day each year everyone celebrates the saint's good deeds. St. Nicholas' name day is December 6.

People all over the world began to celebrate St. Nicholas Day. They hung their stockings by the fire the night before and awoke the next morning to find them filled with candy, fruit, nuts, or toys. St. Nicholas had left a magical gift at each home!

Many years ago, people began to celebrate St. Nicholas' good deeds on Christmas Day, another holiday in December.

St. Nicholas has many names around the world. In some places he is called "Sint Nikolass" or "Sinterklass." Many people know him today as Santa Claus.

A true hero of the people, St. Nicholas still delivers his magical gifts each year at Christmastime. The gifts Santa Claus delivers, gifts of hope and joy, bring the joy of giving to all the children of the world.

Up on the Housetop

B. R. Hanby

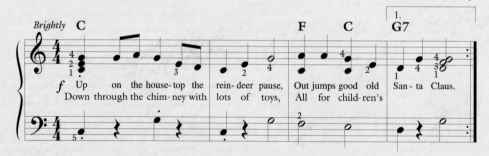

Up on the house-top the rein-deer pause,
Out jumps good old San-ta Claus.
Down through the chim-ney with lots of toys,
All for child-ren's

2. First comes the stocking of little Nell;
Oh, dear Santa fill it well;
Give her a dollie that laughs and cries
One that will open and shut her eyes.

3. Next comes the stocking of little Will;
Oh, just see what a glorious fill!
Here is a hammer and plastic tacks,
Also a ball and a game of jacks.

A Visit From St. Nicholas

Written by Clement C. Moore

Illustrated by Tom Newsom

'Twas the night before Christmas,
        when all through the house
Not a creature was stirring,
        not even a mouse.

The stockings were hung
        by the chimney with care,
In hopes that St. Nicholas
        soon would be there.

The children were nestled
        all snug in their beds,
While visions of sugar-plums
        danced in their heads;

And mama in her kerchief,
    and I in my cap,
Had just settled our brains
    for a long winter's nap,

When out on the lawn
    there arose such a clatter
I sprang from my bed
    to see what was the matter.

Away to the window
    I flew like a flash,
Tore open the shutter,
    and threw up the sash.

The moon on the breast
of the new-fallen snow
Gave a luster of midday
to objects below;

When what to my wondering eyes
should appear
But a miniature sleigh
and eight tiny reindeer,

With a little old driver,
so lively and quick,
I knew in a moment
it must be St. Nick!

More rapid than eagles
his coursers they came,
And he whistled and shouted
and called them by name.

"Now, Dasher! Now, Dancer!
Now, Prancer and Vixen!
On, Comet! On, Cupid!
On, Donder and Blitzen!

To the top of the porch,
to the top of the wall,
Now, dash away, dash away,
dash away all!"

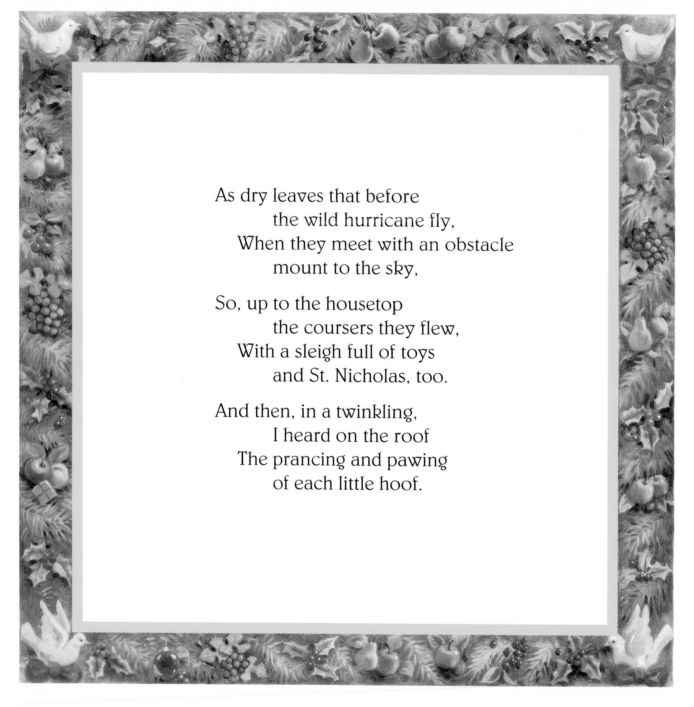

As dry leaves that before
the wild hurricane fly,
When they meet with an obstacle
mount to the sky,

So, up to the housetop
the coursers they flew,
With a sleigh full of toys
and St. Nicholas, too.

And then, in a twinkling,
I heard on the roof
The prancing and pawing
of each little hoof.

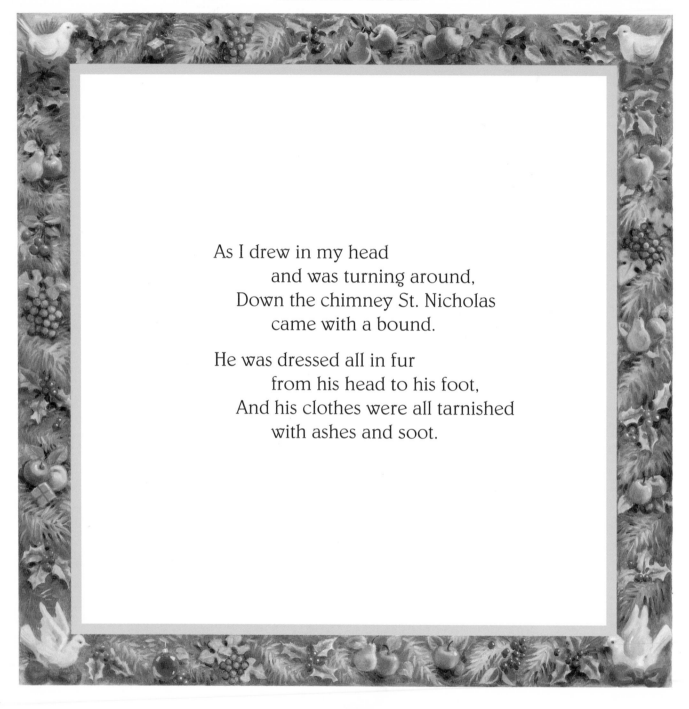

As I drew in my head
    and was turning around,
Down the chimney St. Nicholas
    came with a bound.

He was dressed all in fur
    from his head to his foot,
And his clothes were all tarnished
    with ashes and soot.

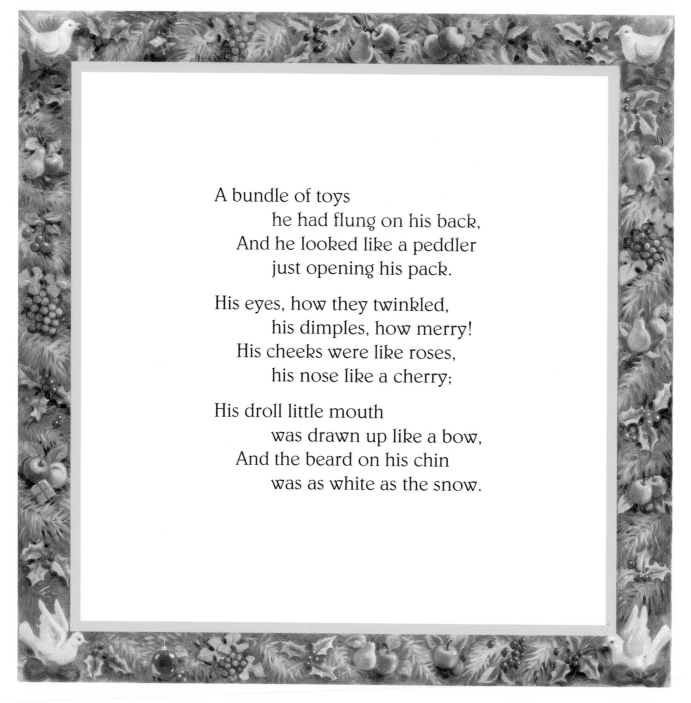

A bundle of toys
      he had flung on his back,
And he looked like a peddler
      just opening his pack.

His eyes, how they twinkled,
      his dimples, how merry!
His cheeks were like roses,
      his nose like a cherry;

His droll little mouth
      was drawn up like a bow,
And the beard on his chin
      was as white as the snow.

The stump of a pipe
    he held tight in his teeth,
And the smoke, it encircled
    his head like a wreath.

He had a broad face
    and a little round belly
That shook, when he laughed,
    like a bowl full of jelly.

He was chubby and plump,
    a right jolly old elf;
And I laughed when I saw him,
    in spite of myself.

A wink of his eye,
      and a twist of his head,
Soon gave me to know
      I had nothing to dread.

He spoke not a word,
      but went straight to his work,
And filled all the stockings,
      then turned with a jerk,

And laying his finger
      aside of his nose,
And giving a nod,
      up the chimney he rose.

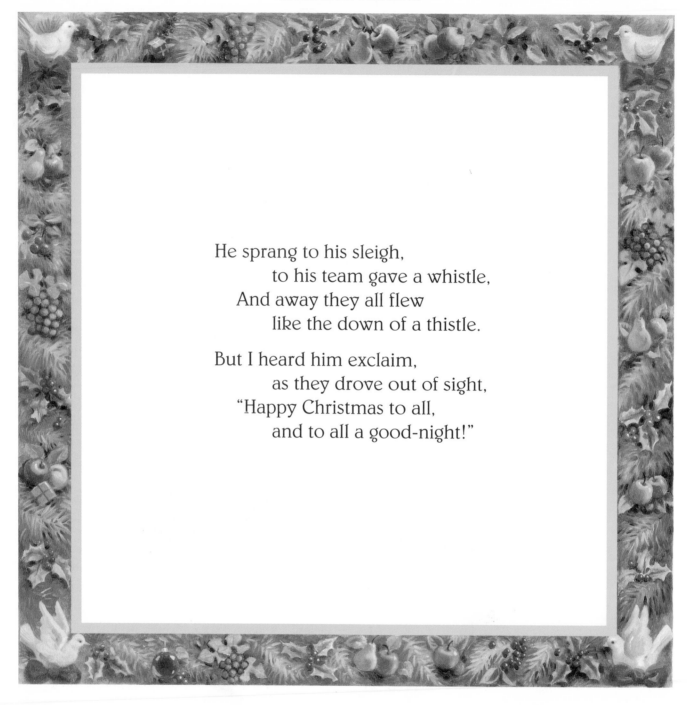

He sprang to his sleigh,
  to his team gave a whistle,
And away they all flew
  like the down of a thistle.

But I heard him exclaim,
  as they drove out of sight,
"Happy Christmas to all,
  and to all a good-night!"

A PONY FOR CHRISTMAS

Originally titled A Miserable, Merry Christmas

Written by Lincoln Steffens
Illustrated by Judith Mitchell

My father's business was one of slow but steady growth. He and his partner were devoted to their families and to "the store," which grew with the town, from a gambling, mining, and ranching community to one of farming, fruit-raising, and building.

As the store made money and I was getting through primary school, my father bought a lot uptown, at Sixteenth and K Streets, and built us a big house. It was off the line of the city's growth, but it was near a new grammar school for me and my sisters, who were coming along quickly after me.

My family was always talking about school, because they had not had much of it themselves, and they thought that they had missed something. My father used to write speeches, my mother verses, and their theory seems to have been that they had talents which a school would have brought to flower. They agreed, therefore, that their children's gift of intelligence should have all the schooling possible.

Now I believed that I had had enough school already, and I was not really interested in traditional studies at all. It interfered with my own business and with my own education.

And indeed I remember very little of the primary school. I learned to read, write, spell, and count, and reading was alright. I had a practical use for books, in which I searched for ideas and parts to play, characters to be, lives to live. The primary school was probably a good one, but I cannot remember learning anything except to read aloud "perfectly" from a teacher who I adored and who was fond of me. She used to embrace me before the whole class, and she favored me openly to the scandal of the other pupils, who called me "teacher's pet." Their scorn did not trouble me. I knew that they envied me.

I paid for her favor, however. When she married I had unhappy feelings of resentment. I didn't want to meet her husband, and when I had to I wouldn't speak to him. He laughed, and she kissed me—happily for her, to me offensively. I never would see her again.

The next year, I fell in love with Miss Kay, another grown young woman who wore glasses and had fine, clear skin. I did not know her. I only saw her in the street. But once I followed her and found out where she lived. After that I would pass her house, hoping to see her. But I would choke with embarrassment if I did.

This fascination lasted for years, and it was still a sort of romance to me when later I was dating a girl nearer my own age.

What interested me in our new neighborhood was not the school, nor the room I was to have in the house all to myself, but the stable which was built in back of the house. My father let me direct the making of a stall, a little smaller than the other stalls, and I prayed and hoped that I would get a pony for Christmas. My father said that someday we might have horses and a cow. Meanwhile, a stable added to the value of a house.

"Someday" is a pain to a boy who lives in and knows only "now." My good little sisters, to comfort me, remarked that Christmas was coming. But Christmas was always coming and grown-ups were always talking about it, asking you what you wanted and then giving you what they wanted you to have. Though everybody knew what I wanted, I told them all again. My mother knew that I told God, too, every night. I wanted a pony, and to make sure that they understood, I declared that I wanted nothing else.

"Nothing but a pony?" my father asked.

"Nothing," I said.

"Not even a pair of high boots?" he asked.

That was hard. I did want boots, but I stuck to the pony. "No, not even boots."

"Nor candy?" he asked again. "There ought to be something to fill your stocking, and Santa Claus can't put a pony into a stocking."

That was true, and he couldn't lead a pony down the chimney, either. But no. "All I want is a pony," I said. "If I can't have a pony, give me nothing."

Now I had been looking myself for the pony I wanted, going to stables and asking many important questions.

"How fast can this one go?" I asked the man at the stables.

"Oh, this one is very fast, indeed," he would say.

Of course, he said this for every pony my father and I approached.

I had seen several that would do, ponies that looked fast and ponies with unique markings. My father let me try riding them. I tried riding so many ponies that I was learning fast to sit a horse. I chose several, but my father always found some fault with them. Soon I was in despair.

When Christmas was at hand I had given up all hope of getting a pony, and on Christmas Eve I hung up my stocking along with my sisters', of whom, by the way, I now had three.

I haven't mentioned them or their coming because, you understand, they were girls, and girls, young girls, counted for nothing in my manly life. They did not mind me either. They were so happy on Christmas Eve that I caught some of their merriment. I speculated on what I would get. I hung up the biggest stocking I had, and we all went reluctantly to bed to wait until morning.

We did not fall asleep right away. We were told that we must not only sleep promptly, but we must not wake up until seven-thirty the next morning. And if we did wake up early, we must not go to the fireplace for our Christmas. This was impossible.

We did fall asleep that night, but we woke up at six o'clock the next morning. We lay in our beds and debated through the open doors whether to obey until, say, half-past six.

Then we all bolted. I don't know who started it, but there was a rush. We all disobeyed. In fact, we raced to disobey and get first to the fireplace in the front room downstairs. And there they were, the gifts, all sorts of wonderful things, mixed-up piles of presents. Only, as I disentangled the mess, I saw that my stocking was empty. It hung limp. Not a thing was in it, under it, or around it. Nothing. My sisters had knelt down, each by her pile of gifts. They were squealing with delight, until they looked up and saw me standing there in my nightgown with nothing. They left their piles to come to me and look with me at my empty place. Nothing. They felt my stocking. Nothing.

I don't remember whether I cried at that moment, but my sisters did. They ran with me back to my bed, and there we all cried until I became indignant. That helped some. I got up, dressed, and drove my sisters away. Then I went alone out into the yard, down to the stable, and there, all by myself, I wept.

My mother came out and found me in my pony stall, sobbing on the floor. She tried to comfort me. But I heard my father outside. He had come partway with her, and she was having some sort of angry quarrel with him. She tried to comfort me and begged me to come to breakfast. I could not. I wanted no comfort and no breakfast. She left me and went on into the house with sharp words for my father.

I do not know what kind of breakfast my family had. My sisters said it was awful, because no one spoke. They were ashamed to enjoy their own toys, so they came to comfort me. But I was rude and ran away from them. I went around to the front of the house, sat down on the steps, and, the crying over, I ached. I was wronged. I was hurt. I can still feel now what I felt then, and I am sure that if one could see the wounds upon our hearts, there would be found still upon mine a scar from that terrible Christmas morning.

And my father, the practical joker, he must have been hurt, too, a little. I saw him looking out the window. He was watching me for an hour or two, drawing back the curtain just a bit, so I wouldn't catch him. But I saw his face, and I think I can see now the anxiety upon it, the worried impatience.

After I don't know how long, surely an hour or two, I was brought to the climax of my agony by the sight of a man riding a pony down the street, a pony wearing a brand-new saddle. It was the most beautiful saddle I had ever seen. I could tell it was a boy's saddle, because the man's feet were not in the stirrups. His legs were too long. This was the realization of all my dreams, the answer to all my prayers. A fine new bridle, with a light bit. And the pony!

As he drew near, I saw that the pony was really a small horse, what we called an Indian pony, a bay, with black mane and tail, and one white foot and a white star on his forehead. I would have given anything for a horse like that, and I could have forgiven anyone for anything.

But the man came along slowly, reading the numbers on the houses, and as my impossible hopes rose, he looked at our door and passed by, he and the pony, and the saddle and the bridle. It was too much. I fell upon the steps, and broke into such a flood of tears. I was a floating wreck when, suddenly, I heard a voice.

"Say, kid," it said, "do you know a boy named Lennie Steffens?"

I looked up. The voice had come from the man riding the pony, and he was back at our house.

"Yes," I sputtered through my tears. "That's me."

"Well," he said, "then this is your horse. I've been looking all over for you and your house. Why don't you put your number where it can be seen?"

My horse? I couldn't believe it. The man was riding my horse! "Get down," I said, running out to him.

He went on saying something about how he "should have been here at seven o'clock. Your father told me to bring the horse here and tie him to your post and leave him for you and . . ."

"Get down," I said again, as I reached the horse.

I was about to pull him off the horse when he finally got down. Then he boosted me up to that saddle. He offered to fit the stirrups for me, but I didn't want him to. I wanted to ride.

"What's the matter with you?" he said angrily. "What are you crying for? Don't you like the horse? He's a dandy, this horse. I've known him for a long time."

I hardly heard him, because I could scarcely wait to ride that horse. But the man persisted. He adjusted the stirrups, and then finally off I rode slowly at a walk, so happy, so thrilled, that I did not know what I was doing. I did not look back at the house or the man. I rode up the street, taking note of everything, of the reins, of the pony's long mane, of the carved leather saddle. I had never seen anything so beautiful. And it was mine!

I rode past my neighbors' houses and waved to the people outside. I rode over the bridge, past the school, and around the fire station twice. I was going to ride past Miss Kay's house, but I looked down and noticed on the horn of the saddle some stains like raindrops. I quickly turned around and trotted home to the stable. There was my family, my father, my mother, and my sisters, all working for me, all happy. They had been putting in place the tools of my new hobby—blankets, currycombs, brushes, pitchfork, everything, and there was hay in the loft.

"What did you come back so soon for?" my mother asked. "Why didn't you go on riding?"

I pointed to the stains. "I wasn't going to get my new saddle rained on," I said.

And my father laughed. "It isn't raining," he said. "Those are not raindrops."

"They are tears," my mother gasped, and she gave my father a look which sent him off to the house. Worse still, my mother offered to wipe away the tears still running out of my eyes. I gave her such a look as she had given him, and she went off after my father, drying her own tears.

My sisters stayed, and we all unsaddled the pony, put on his halter, led him to his stall, and fed him. It began to really rain then, so all the rest of that memorable day we combed that pony. The girls braided his mane, forelock, and tail, while I pitchforked hay to him and brushed his soft coat. For a change, we brought him out to drink. We led him up and down, blanketed like a racehorse. Then we took turns at that. But the best fun was to clean him.

When we went reluctantly to our midday Christmas dinner, we all smelled of horse, and my sisters had to wash their faces and hands. I was asked to, but I refused, until my mother begged me to look in the mirror. Then I washed up quickly. My face was caked with the muddy lines of tears that had coursed over my cheeks to my mouth. Having washed away that shame, I ate my dinner. As I ate, I grew hungrier and hungrier. It was my first meal that day, and as I filled up on the turkey and the stuffing, the cranberries and the pies, the fruit and the nuts, I could laugh. My mother said I still choked and sobbed now and then, but I laughed, too. I saw and enjoyed my sisters' presents until I had to go out and attend to my pony, who was there, really and truly there. And I went and looked to make sure that the saddle and the bridle were there, too.

But that Christmas, which my father had planned so carefully, was it the best or the worst I ever knew? He often asked me that. I could never answer as a boy. I think now that it was both. It covered the whole distance from broken-hearted misery to bursting happiness. A grown-up could hardly have stood it.

CHRISTMAS IN SWEDEN

Written by Sarah Toast   Illustrated by Jane McIlvain and Winky Adam

It is dark, cold, and snowy in Sweden in December. The days are short and the nights long. Families begin the Christmas season by attending church on the first Sunday of Advent, which is the fourth Sunday before Christmas. The children count the days from the first day of December until Christmas with an Advent calendar. Each morning, they open a flap in the calendar's Christmas scene to see the charming picture behind it.

But the Christmas festivities really begin on December 13 with St. Lucia's Day, which celebrates the patron saint of light. The eldest daughter gets up before dawn and dresses as the "Queen of Light" in a long white dress. She wears a crown of leaves and lighted candles. Singing "Santa Lucia," the Lucia Queen goes to every bedroom to serve coffee and treats to each member of the family. The younger children in the family help, too.

Many families go to the Christmas market in the old medieval section of Stockholm to buy handmade toys, ornaments, and candy. Gift-givers like to seal the package with sealing wax and write a special verse that will accompany the gift.

The whole family helps to select the Christmas tree just a day or two before Christmas. Then they use papier-mâché apples, heart-shaped paper baskets filled with candies, gilded pinecones, small straw goats and pigs, little Swedish flags, glass ornaments, and small figures of gnomes wearing red hats to decorate the tree.

The delightful smells of gingerbread cookies in the shape of hearts, stars, or goats fill the house. Many families set out a sheaf of grain on a pole for hungry birds.

At the midday meal on Christmas Eve, families follow the tradition of "dipping in the kettle." To remember a time when food was scarce in Sweden, the family eats bread dipped into a kettle of thin broth.

After this modest beginning, they enjoy a bountiful *smörgasbord* of *lutefisk*, which is dried fish, Christmas ham, boiled potatoes, pork sausage, herring salad, spiced breads, and many different kinds of sweets. It is said that whoever finds the almond in the special rice pudding will marry in the coming year.

After dinner, the Christmas tree lights are lit. Then the *Jultomten*, the tiny Christmas gnome, comes on a sleigh drawn by the Christmas goat, *Julbokar*. In some families, a friend or family member dresses up in a red robe and wears a long white beard to bring toys for the children. In other families, the *Jultomten's* gifts are left beneath the tree. After the gifts are opened, the family dances around the tree singing a special song.

In the predawn darkness of Christmas Day, candles illuminate every window. Bells ring out, calling families to churches lit by candlelight. Back home again, the parents kindle a blaze in the fireplace to light the darkness. The following day is Second Day Christmas, a day of singing carols.

On January 5, the eve of Twelfth Night, or Epiphany, young boys dress up as the Wise Men and carry a lighted candle on a pole topped with a star. These boys go from house to house singing carols.

Then on St. Knut's Day on January 13, there is one last Christmas party. The grown-ups pack away the Christmas decorations while the costumed children eat the last of the wrapped candies left on the tree. Then out goes the tree to the tune of the last song of Christmas.

Jingle Bells

J. Pierpont

THE NUTCRACKER

Written by E. T. A. Hoffmann
Illustrated by Doris Ettlinger

On the twenty-fourth of December, Dr. Stahlbaum's children were not allowed to set foot in the family parlor. Fritz and Marie sat together in the back room and waited. In whispers Fritz told his younger sister that he had seen Godfather Drosselmeier. At that, Marie clapped her little hands for joy and cried out, "Oh, what do you think Godfather Drosselmeier has made for us?"

Fritz said it was a fortress, with all kinds of soldiers marching up and down.

"No, no," Marie interrupted. "Mr. Drosselmeier said something to me about a beautiful garden with a big lake in it and lovely swans swimming all around on it."

"Mr. Drosselmeier can't make a whole garden," said Fritz rather rudely.

Then the children tried to guess what their parents would give them. Marie sat deep in thought, while Fritz muttered, "I'd like a chestnut horse and some soldiers."

At that moment, a bell rang, the doors flew open, and a flood of light streamed in from the big parlor. "Come in, dear children," said Papa and Mama.

The children stood silently with shining eyes. Then Marie cried out, "Oh, how lovely!" And Fritz took two rather spectacular jumps into the air.

Marie discovered a silk dress hanging on the tree. "What a lovely dress!" she cried.

Meanwhile, Fritz galloped around the table, trying out the new horse he had found. Then he reviewed his new squadron of soldiers, who were admirably outfitted in red and gold uniforms.

Just then, the bell rang again. Knowing that Godfather Drosselmeier would be unveiling his present, the children ran to the table that had been set up beside the wall. The screen that had hidden it was taken away. The children saw a magnificent castle with dozens of sparkling windows and golden towers. Chimes played as tiny ladies and gentlemen strolled around the rooms, and children in little skirts danced to the music of the chimes.

Fritz looked at the beautiful castle, then said, "Godfather Drosselmeier, let me go inside your castle."

"Impossible," said Mr. Drosselmeier.

"Then make the children come out," cried Fritz.

"No," said their godfather crossly, "that, too, is impossible. This is how the mechanism works, and it cannot be changed."

"Then I don't really care for it," said Fritz. "My soldiers march as I command, and they're not shut up in a house." Fritz marched away to play with his soldiers.

Marie did not leave the Christmas table, for she was well-behaved.

The real reason why Marie did not want to leave the Christmas table was that she had just caught sight of something. When Fritz marched away, an excellent little man came into view.

The distinction of his dress showed him to be a man of taste and breeding. Oddly enough, though, he wore a skimpy cloak that was made of wood. His light green eyes were full of kindness, and his white-cotton beard was most becoming.

"Oh, Father dear," Marie cried out, "who does the dear little man belong to?"

"Dear child," said Dr. Stahlbaum, "our friend here will serve you all well. He will crack hard nuts for all of you with his teeth."

Carefully picking him up from the table, Dr. Stahlbaum lifted his wooden cloak, and the little man opened his mouth wide, revealing two rows of sharp white teeth. At her father's bidding, Marie put in a nut, and—*crack*—the little man bit it in two, the shell fell down, and Marie found the sweet kernel in her hand.

Fritz ran over to his sister. He chose the biggest nut, and all of a sudden—*crack, crack*—three little teeth fell out of the Nutcracker's mouth.

"Oh, my poor little Nutcracker!" Marie cried, taking him out of Fritz's hands.

"He's just a stupid fool," said Fritz. "He calls himself a nutcracker, and his teeth are no good. Give him to me, Marie."

Marie was in tears. "No, no!" she cried. "He's my dear Nutcracker and you can't have him." Sobbing, Marie wrapped the Nutcracker in her little handkerchief. She bandaged his wounded mouth. Then she rocked him in her arms like a baby.

It was getting late, and Mother urged her children to turn in for the night. But Marie pleaded, "Just a little while longer, Mother dear."

Marie's mother put out all of the candles, leaving on only one lamp. "Go to bed soon," she said, "or you won't be able to get up tomorrow."

As soon as Marie was alone, she set the Nutcracker carefully on the table, unwrapped the handkerchief ever so slowly, and examined his wounds.

"Dear Nutcracker," she said softly, "don't be angry at my brother, Fritz. He meant no harm. I'm going to take care of you until you're well and happy again."

Marie picked up the Nutcracker and placed him next to the other toys in a glass cabinet in the parlor. She shut the door and was going to her bedroom, when she heard whispering and shuffling. The clock whirred twelve times. Then she heard giggling and squeaking all around her, followed by the sound of a thousand little feet scampering behind the walls. Soon Marie saw mice all over the room, and in the end they formed ranks, just as Fritz's soldiers did.

Crushed stone flew out of the floor as though driven by some underground force, and seven mouse heads with seven sparkling crowns rose up, squeaking and squealing hideously. This enormous mouse was hailed by the entire army, cheering with three loud squeaks. And then the army set itself in motion—*hop, hop, trot, trot*—heading straight for the toy cabinet.

At the same time, Marie saw a strange glow inside the toy cabinet. All at once, Nutcracker jumped from the cabinet, and the squeaking and squealing started again.

"Trusty Vassal-Drummer," cried the Nutcracker, "sound the advance!" The drummer played so loudly that the windows of the toy cabinet rattled. A clattering was heard from inside, and all the boxes containing Fritz's army bursted open. Soldiers climbed out and jumped to the bottom shelf. Then they formed ranks on the floor. The Nutcracker ran back and forth, shouting words of encouragement to the troops.

A few moments later, guns were going *boom*! *boom*! The mice advanced and overran some of the artillery positions. Such was the confusion, and such were the smoke and dust, that Marie could hardly see what was going on. But this much was certain—both sides fought with grim determination, and for a long while victory hung in the balance. Then the mice brought up more troops.

The Nutcracker found himself trapped against the toy cabinet. "Bring up the reserves!" he cried. And true enough, a few men came out, but they wielded their swords so clumsily that they knocked off General Nutcracker's cap.

The Nutcracker was in dire peril. He tried to jump over the ledge of the toy cabinet, but his legs were too short. In wild despair he shouted, "A horse, a horse! My kingdom for a horse!"

At that moment, the King of Mice charged the Nutcracker. Without quite knowing what she was doing, Marie took off her left shoe and flung it with all her might, hoping to hit the Mice King. At that moment, everything vanished from Marie's sight. She felt a sharp pain in her left arm and fell to the floor in a faint.

When Marie awoke from her deep sleep, she was lying in her own little bed. The sun shining into the room sparkled on the ice-coated windowpanes. A strange gentleman was sitting beside her, but she soon recognized him as Dr. Wendelstern. "She's awake," he said softly to Marie's mother. She came over and gave Marie an anxious look.

"Oh, Mother dear," Marie whispered. "Have all the nasty mice gone away? Was the Nutcracker saved?"

"Don't talk such nonsense, child," said her mother. "What have mice got to do with the Nutcracker? Oh, we've been so worried about you. Last night, I went into the living room and found you lying beside the glass toy cabinet in a faint, bleeding terribly. The Nutcracker was lying on your arm, and your left shoe was lying on the floor nearby..."

"Oh, Mother," Marie broke in. "There had just been a big battle between the dolls and the mice. The mice were going to capture the poor Nutcracker. So I threw my shoe at the mice, and after that I don't know what happened."

Marie's father came in and had a long talk with Dr. Wendelstern. Marie had to stay in bed and take medicine for a week.

Then Godfather Drosselmeier came to visit. "I've brought you something that will give you pleasure," he told Marie. With that, he reached into his pocket and took out the Nutcracker, whose lost teeth he had put back in very neatly and firmly, and whose broken jaw he had fixed as good as new. Marie cried out for joy!

That night, Marie was awakened in the moonlight by a strange rumbling. "Oh, dear, the mice are here again!" Marie cried out in fright.

Then she saw the King of Mice squeeze through the hole in the wall. He scurried across the floor and jumped onto the table beside Marie's bed. "Give me your candy," he said, "or I'll bite your Nutcracker to pieces." Then he slipped back into the hole.

Marie was so frightened that she could hardly say a word. That night she put her whole supply of delicacies at the foot of the toy cabinet. The next morning the candy was gone.

Marie was happy because she had saved the Nutcracker, but that night the Mouse King returned. "Give me your beautiful dress and all your picture books," he hissed.

Marie was beside herself with anguish. The next morning she went to the toy cabinet sobbing and said to the Nutcracker, "Oh, dear, what can I do? If I give that horrid Mouse King all my books and my dress, he'll just keep asking for more."

The Nutcracker said in a strained whisper, "Just get me a sword . . ." At that his words ebbed away, and his eyes became fixed.

Marie asked Fritz for a sword, and Fritz slung it around the Nutcracker's waist.

The next night fear and dread kept Marie awake. At the stroke of twelve she heard clanging and crashing in the parlor. And then suddenly, "Squeak!"

Soon Marie heard a soft knocking at the door and a faint little voice, "Miss Stahlbaum, open the door and have no fear. I bring good news!" Marie swiftly opened the door and found that the Nutcracker had turned into a prince!

The prince took Marie's hand and told her how he was really Godfather Drosselmeier's nephew, and an evil spell had turned him into a nutcracker. When he defeated the Mouse King, the spell was broken and he was turned back into a prince.

"Oh, Miss Stahlbaum," said the prince, "what splendid things I can show you in this hour of victory over my enemy, if you will follow me a little way."

Marie agreed and followed the prince to the big clothes cupboard in the entrance hall. The door of the cupboard was wide open. The prince stepped inside, pulled a tassel, and a little ladder came down through the sleeve of a traveling coat.

Marie climbed the ladder and soon passed through the sleeve. When she looked out through the neck hole, she found herself in a fragrant meadow.

"This is Candy Meadow," said the prince.

Looking up, Marie saw a beautiful arch as they were passing through it. "Oh, it's so wonderful here," she sighed.

The prince clapped his hands, and several little shepherds appeared. They brought up a golden chair and asked Marie to sit down. Then the shepherds danced a charming ballet. Suddenly, as if at a signal, they all vanished into the woods.

The prince took Marie's hand and led her down Honey River. Downstream there was a sweet little village. "This is Gingerbread City," said the prince. "The people who live here are beautiful, but most are dreadfully cranky because they have awful toothaches. But instead of worrying our heads over that, let's sail across the lake to the capital."

The prince clapped his hands. The gondola appeared in the distance and quickly came closer. Marie and the prince stepped onto the gondola, which quickly started off again.

Soon Marie found herself near a marvelous city. "This," said Nutcracker, "is the capital." The city was so beautiful and splendorous. Not only were the walls and towers of the most magnificent colors, but the shapes of the buildings were like nothing else on earth.

Suddenly, Marie saw a castle with a hundred lofty towers. "This," said the prince, "is Marzipan Castle." At that moment soft music was heard, the gates of the castle opened, and out stepped four ladies so richly and splendidly attired that Marie knew they could only be princesses. One by one, they embraced their brother.

The ladies led Marie and the prince to an inner room, whose walls were made of sparkling colored crystal. The princesses planned to prepare a meal for Marie and the prince. They brought in the most wonderful fruit and candy Marie had ever seen and began to squeeze the fruit and grate the sugared almonds.

The most beautiful of the prince's sisters handed her a little golden mortar and said, "Dear sweet friend, would you care to pound some rock candy?"

While Marie pounded away, the prince told the history of the cruel war between the Mouse King's army and his own.

As Marie listened to his story, she began to feel very dizzy. Soon Marie felt as though she were falling.

Marie fell to the floor. When she opened her eyes, she was lying in her little bed, and her mother was standing there.

"How can anyone sleep so long!" her mother exclaimed.

"Oh, Mother," said Marie, "you cannot imagine all of the places that young Mr. Drosselmeier took me to last night."

Marie's mother looked at her in amazement. "You've had a long, beautiful dream, but now you must forget all that nonsense," she said.

"But, Mother dear," said Marie, "I know that the Nutcracker is really young Mr. Drosselmeier from Nuremberg, Godfather Drosselmeier's nephew."

Mrs. Stahlbaum burst out laughing. Marie was on the verge of tears. Her mother sternly said, "You're to forget about this foolishness once and for all." So she did.

One day Marie's mother came into her room and said, "Your godfather's nephew from Nuremberg is here. So be on your good behavior."

Marie turned as red as a beet when she saw the young man, and she turned even redder when young Drosselmeier asked her to go with him to the cabinet in the parlor.

He went down on one knee and said, "Miss Stahlbaum, you see at your feet the happiest of men, whose life you saved on this very spot. Please come and reign with me over Marzipan Castle."

Marie said softly, "Of course I will come with you."

Marie left in a golden carriage. And she is still the queen of a country where the most wonderful things can be seen if you have the right sort of eyes for it.

Dance of the Sugar Plum Fairy

Rhythmically and Delicately
2nd time play both hands one octave higher

Tchaikovsky
from *The Nutcracker Suite*

Toyland

Words: Glen MacDonough

Music: Victor Herbert
from *Babes in Toyland*

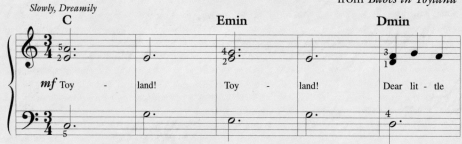

Slowly, Dreamily

mf Toy - land! Toy - land! Dear lit - tle

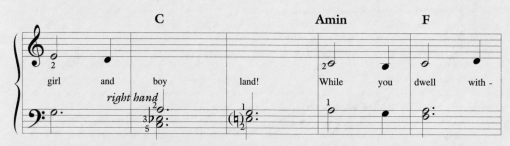

girl and boy land! While you dwell with -

right hand

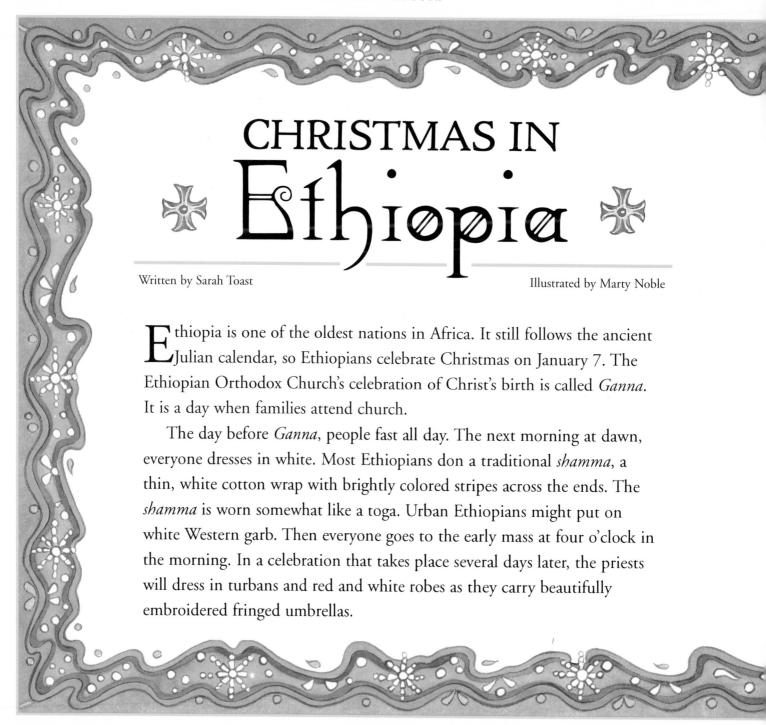

CHRISTMAS IN
Ethiopia

Written by Sarah Toast

Illustrated by Marty Noble

Ethiopia is one of the oldest nations in Africa. It still follows the ancient Julian calendar, so Ethiopians celebrate Christmas on January 7. The Ethiopian Orthodox Church's celebration of Christ's birth is called *Ganna*. It is a day when families attend church.

The day before *Ganna*, people fast all day. The next morning at dawn, everyone dresses in white. Most Ethiopians don a traditional *shamma*, a thin, white cotton wrap with brightly colored stripes across the ends. The *shamma* is worn somewhat like a toga. Urban Ethiopians might put on white Western garb. Then everyone goes to the early mass at four o'clock in the morning. In a celebration that takes place several days later, the priests will dress in turbans and red and white robes as they carry beautifully embroidered fringed umbrellas.

282

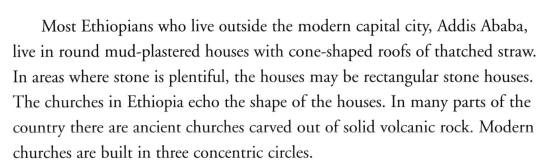

Most Ethiopians who live outside the modern capital city, Addis Ababa, live in round mud-plastered houses with cone-shaped roofs of thatched straw. In areas where stone is plentiful, the houses may be rectangular stone houses. The churches in Ethiopia echo the shape of the houses. In many parts of the country there are ancient churches carved out of solid volcanic rock. Modern churches are built in three concentric circles.

In a modern church, the choir assembles in the outer circle. Each person entering the church is given a candle. The congregation walks around the church three times in a solemn procession, holding the flickering candles. Then they gather in the second circle to stand throughout the long mass, with the men and boys separated from the women and girls. The center circle is the holiest space in the church, where the priest serves Holy Communion.

Around the time of *Ganna*, the men and boys play a game that is also called *ganna*. It is somewhat like hockey, played with a curved stick and a round wooden ball.

The foods enjoyed during the Christmas season include *wat*, a thick, spicy stew of meat, vegetables, and sometimes eggs as well. The *wat* is served from a beautifully decorated watertight basket onto a "plate" of *injerá*, which is flat sourdough bread. Pieces of *injerá* are used as an edible spoon to scoop up the *wat*.

Twelve days after *Ganna*, on January 19, Ethiopians begin the three-day celebration called *Timkat*, which commemorates the baptism of Christ. The children walk to church services in a procession. They wear the crowns and robes of the church youth groups they belong to. The grown-ups wear the *shamma*. The priests will now wear their red and white robes and carry embroidered fringed umbrellas.

The music of Ethiopian instruments makes the *Timkat* procession a very festive event. The *sistrum* is a percussion instrument with tinkling metal disks. A long, T-shaped prayer stick called a *makamiya* taps out the walking beat and also serves as a support for the priest during the long church service that follows. Church officials called *dabtaras* study hard to learn the musical chants, *melekets*, for the ceremony.

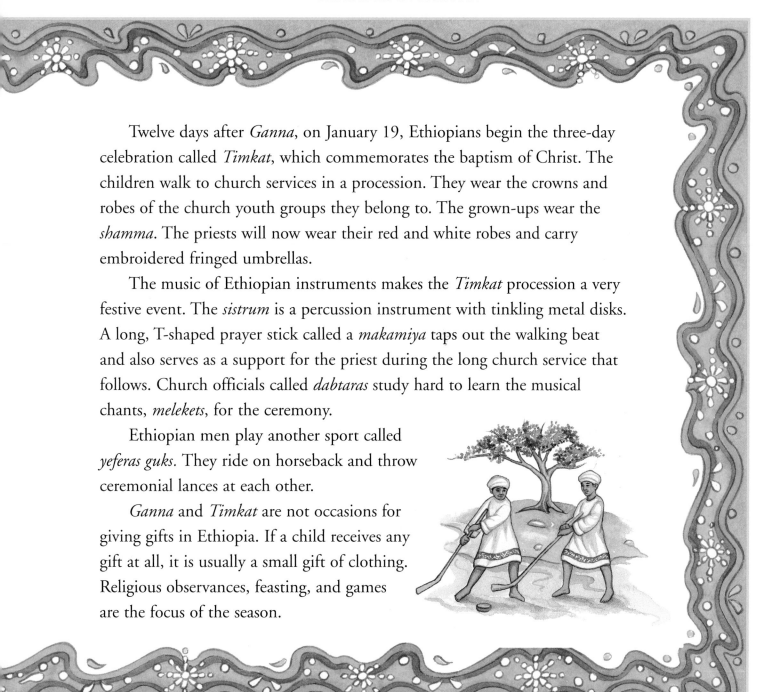

Ethiopian men play another sport called *yeferas guks*. They ride on horseback and throw ceremonial lances at each other.

Ganna and *Timkat* are not occasions for giving gifts in Ethiopia. If a child receives any gift at all, it is usually a small gift of clothing. Religious observances, feasting, and games are the focus of the season.

THE THREE SKATERS

Adapted by Lynne Suesse
Illustrated by Linda Graves

In the faraway land of Holland, a baker sadly closed up his shop. He carried a worn sack with a few loaves of bread. Not many people came into the bakery that day, because times were hard and people did not have extra money for fresh bread. The baker had to bring home the leftovers so that they would not go to waste.

"Maybe I can make a nice bread pudding with these loaves," said the baker to himself. "It would be a shame not to use such delicious bread." The baker walked off into the cold, gray afternoon.

The baker's mind drifted to visions of his family. He pictured them all warm and snug by the fireplace, waiting for his arrival. He knew his wife would be a little disappointed with the sales at the bakery, but she would take the loaves of bread and cheerfully make the best of them. He smiled beneath the scratchy wool of his scarf. His eyes watered, from the icy wind and from the joy that his family brought to him.

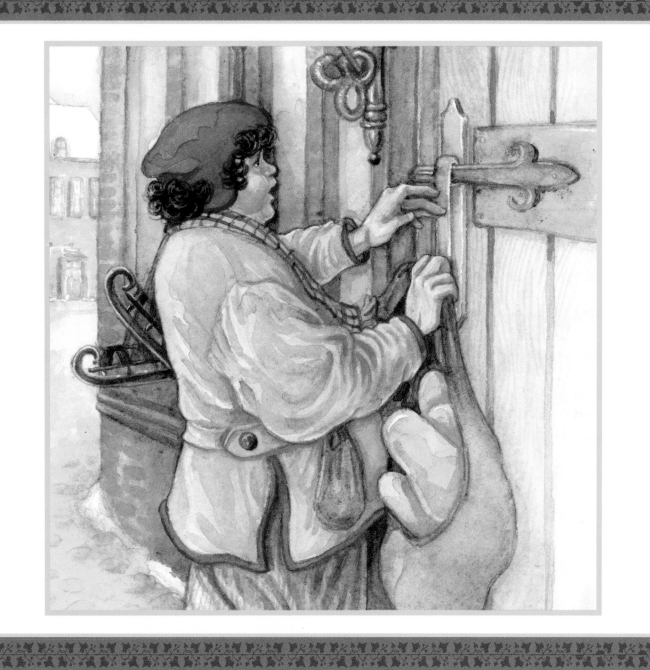

The baker blinked the tears away and kept walking. When he reached the frozen canal, he sat down upon a log and strapped his wooden skates to his feet. As he secured the straps, he looked down the icy canal. The land seemed to stretch out endlessly before him. The air was crisp and the wind was bitter. The baker shivered and pulled his scarf higher on his face.

About a half-mile down the canal, the baker could see the farmer coming toward him. Soon he was joined by the farmer, who was also his neighbor. He, too, carried a sack. The two men greeted each other quietly and began skating together. Their skates soon fell into a rhythm.

"Have you been to the market today?" asked the baker.

The farmer nodded slowly. "Not much luck, though," he said.

"Same here. I still have a few loaves of bread," said the baker. He turned his gaze down the canal and continued to skate.

The farmer also could not wait to be home with his family. He looked forward to warming himself by the fire and playing with his children. His youngest child, Lily, had been ill, and the farmer wanted to get her something special at the market. But he did not sell many apples and had to bring a sack of them back home.

"Perhaps a nice apple pie will warm little Lily and make her smile," said the farmer to himself.

Times were tough for everyone. It was clear that both men did not need to say much to each other. They knew exactly how the other one felt.

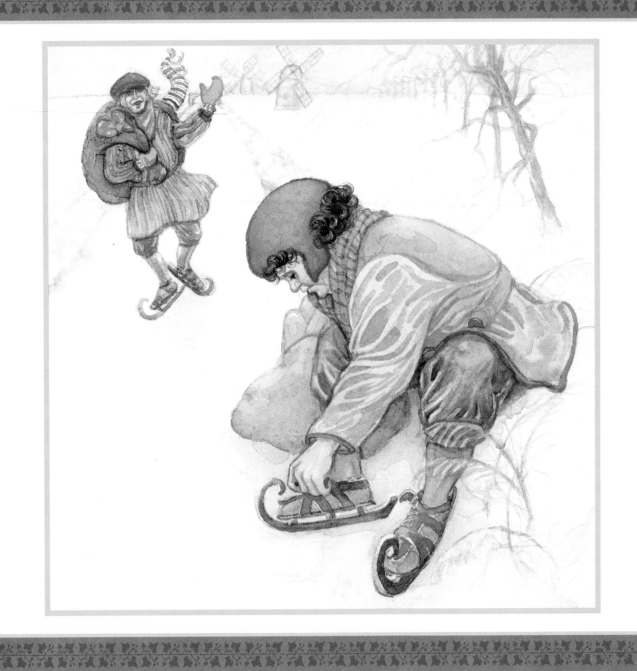

As they continued to skate, the clouds grew thicker. The two men wanted to get home as quickly as possible. Soon they came to where another canal met up with theirs. They could see another figure coming toward them from the other canal. With a wave, they saw that it was their friend, the weaver.

"Hello, gentlemen," said the weaver. He skated right up to the farmer and the baker. They greeted the weaver warmly, and they all began to skate together. Now the sound of the three men's skates was all that could be heard on the smooth ice of the canal.

The weaver had also come from the market, where he had been trying to sell the beautiful blankets he had woven. Since no one had any extra money to spend, the weaver left the market with all of his blankets and no money. He tried to keep his spirits up, however, by taking pride in knowing that his blankets were beautifully crafted and woven out of love.

"It will be wonderful when we get home and out of the chill," said the weaver, trying to start some cheerful conversation.

The other two men just nodded their heads in agreement. Their thick scarves and the biting wind made it hard to talk to one another. They continued along the canal in silence.

As they passed an abandoned farm, the weaver suddenly stopped skating. He turned his gaze toward the old rundown barn in the middle of the field. He thought he heard an unusual noise.

"Stop! Listen!" the weaver called to his companions.

The farmer and the baker quickly stopped. They returned to the spot where the weaver was standing.

The three men stood on the icy canal, staring at the old barn. Suddenly a slice of sunlight split through the clouds and shone brightly onto the barn. It was a most unusual sight!

"Listen. Do you hear that?" asked the weaver.

The farmer and the baker held their breath and listened. All at once, the three men heard the familiar sound of a baby crying. It seemed to be coming from the old barn, now cast in an eerie glow.

"It sounds like a child," said the farmer.

"But how could it be? That farm has been abandoned for years," said the weaver.

"Perhaps a lamb was left in the barn," said the baker. "It sounds like a lamb."

The three men heard the sound again and knew in an instant that it was not a lamb. It sounded, most definitely, like a child.

Without another word, all three men stepped off the ice and into the snow. They took off their skates and began walking toward the barn. As they reached the doorway, they could hear the baby's cries beginning to soften as the gentle sound of a mother's voice sang a soulful lullaby. The men opened the barn door without knocking. It was as if they knew that it was alright—that whoever was inside wanted them to come in.

Inside the barn, thin beams of sunlight streamed through the holes in the roof and walls. There was not a lamb that had been abandoned by the barn's owner, but the scene inside the barn was most incredible. In the center of the barn sat a young woman holding a newborn infant. She was singing the most beautiful and unusual lullaby. She stopped singing as she looked up at the men. Then she smiled.

The men could not help but smile shyly back at the new mother. They were very surprised that anyone was in the abandoned barn, but even more surprised to see a lovely young mother holding a newborn infant. The three men looked around the barn and saw a man raking hay in a stall. The man looked very tired. After a moment, he stopped his chore and addressed the three strangers.

"It's not much of a home, but we had nowhere else to go," he explained. "We are on our way to visit relatives. My wife had the baby before we could reach our destination."

The farmer, the baker, and the weaver all turned back to look at the mother and her newborn baby.

"Are your relatives expecting your arrival?" asked the weaver.

"Yes, but traveling will be difficult now with the infant. We can't stay here long, though. We have no food, and it is very cold and drafty inside this barn," the man said. He then finished raking a soft pile of hay and laid down a thin piece of cloth on top. Then the man walked over to the mother, took the baby, and placed it on its makeshift bed.

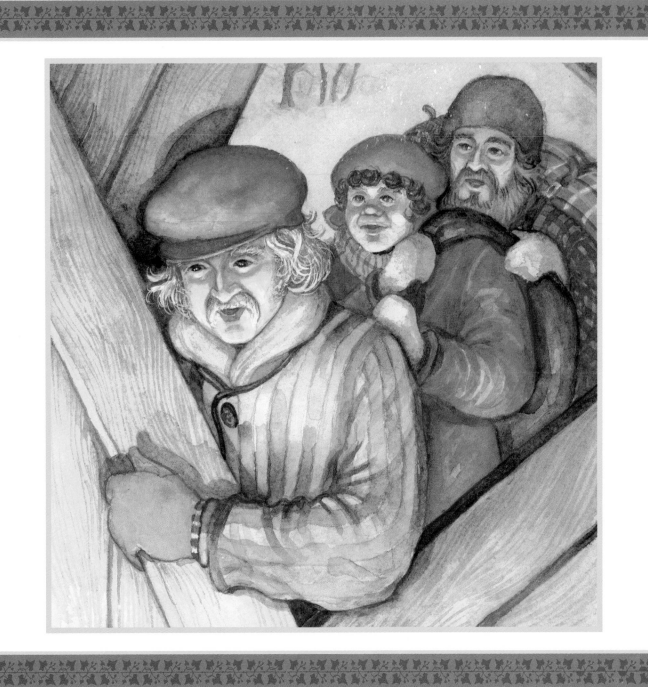

The mother and father gathered around the child. It was obvious to the men that the young family was happy despite their hardship. The man and woman looked lovingly at each other and their new baby.

The family scene touched the three men and, all at once, they took their items from their sacks and laid them on the floor near the child's bed. They smiled at the family, then quietly left the drafty barn. Without a word, the farmer, the baker, and the weaver walked through the snow to the edge of the canal. They bent down to put on their skates, then skated off once again.

Now all three of the men's sacks were empty. They did not seem concerned with coming home empty-handed, however. They felt in their hearts that what they had done was right. Once again, the only sound to be heard was their skates on the ice.

As he skated, the baker thought of his home. The mother and child reminded him of his wife and children waiting to see him walk through the door. He felt blessed knowing that they were safe and warm in their small, but cozy house.

The farmer's thoughts drifted to his sick daughter. How fragile and tiny she looked when he left her that morning, bundled up in her blanket. He thought of the newborn child and how fragile it looked in its young mother's arms. He said a blessing for the young family left alone in that old barn.

The weaver's prayers also went out to the mother and her child. He hoped that his handmade blankets would provide enough warmth and shelter for the family until they could continue on their journey.

The three men were so deep in thought that they did not notice their sacks getting heavier. Slowly each sack was filling, as if someone was dropping items into each one. But the men did not perceive the growing heaviness. They did notice, however, that they were nearing the village where they all lived. A smile crossed each of their lips, because they knew that they would be home soon. It had been a truly strange, but amazing day.

As they reached the edge of town, the three men stepped off the ice. The crisp snow crunched under their skates. They still did not speak to one another. Each one took off his skates and slung them over his shoulders. Their sacks were quite full by this time, but still not one man made mention of it.

The farmer said good-bye to the baker and the weaver and headed toward his home. The baker and weaver also said their good-byes and parted company. It had been an unusual day, but neither the farmer, the baker, nor the weaver felt like talking. It was as if they all knew what the other one was thinking.

By the time the baker reached his front door, his sack was brimming and very heavy. He walked into his home and found his family just as he had pictured, all huddled around the warmth of the fireplace. When they saw him come through the door, all the children shouted at once, "Daddy! Daddy! Daddy's home!"

His wife walked over to the baker and gave him a warm hug. That is when she noticed the sack he was carrying. "Oh, dear! What a day at the shop!" she said, her eyes wide with wonder.

The baker put down the sack. Immediately cookies and cakes, hams and bread, teas and spices, fruits and vegetables came flooding out! There were also wrapped presents for everyone. The whole family began to cry with delight.

"Oh, Daddy! How wonderful!" cried the baker's daughter.

"Dear, we are blessed!" cried the baker's wife.

The baker had no idea how his sack got so full with such wonderful gifts, but he knew it must have something to do with the amazing scene in the barn.

That night the baker and his family had the best dinner ever. Not only did they have enough for that night, but for forty nights after!

When it was time for bed, the baker gathered the children in front of the fire and told them the amazing story of the family in the old barn on the abandoned field. He described how the sunlight broke through the clouds and shone only on the little barn where they were staying.

"It was a wonderful sight, indeed!" he told the children.

After he put his family to bed with full bellies and wondrous visions in their heads, the baker sat up and looked out the window. He thought of the farmer and the weaver. He knew that their night was as joyous and amazing as his had been. There was no need to wonder. For all three men had witnessed the same miracle. They all gave everything they had out of pure generosity and the goodness of their hearts. And even though the winter winds howled outside, it was the warmest night the farmer, the baker, and the weaver had ever had.

CHRISTMAS IN

Holland

Written by Sarah Toast   Illustrated by Jane McIlvain

Dutch children in Holland, or the Netherlands, anxiously look forward to St. Nicholas Day on December 6. While they eagerly await the arrival of *Sinterklaas*, the people around them shop for gifts, write a little poem to accompany each one, and carefully wrap each gift to keep the contents a surprise to the receiver.

Sinterklaas is a kindly bishop. He wears red robes and a tall, pointed mitre on his head. *Sinterklaas* travels by ship from Spain to Amsterdam's harbor every winter. With him he brings his white horse and a huge sack full of gifts for the children. The mayor and all the people of Amsterdam flock to the harbor to greet *Sinterklaas* as he arrives. Bells ring out, the people cheer, and a brass band leads a parade through the streets. The parade stops at the royal palace, where the Queen welcomes *Sinterklaas*.

Families celebrate St. Nicholas Eve at home with lots of good food, hot chocolate, and a *letterbanket*. This is a "letter cake" made in the shape of the first letter of the family's last name. In some families, each person gets a little *letterbanket* with their first initial.

Then out come the carefully chosen and wrapped "surprises." Every gift is accompanied by a personal verse written by the giver about the recipient. And even though the gifts are from family and friends, they all are signed "*Sinterklaas*." No one is supposed to know who really gave the gift. The way they are wrapped adds to the surprise. A small gift might be hidden in a potato. A big gift might be kept a surprise by being hidden in the attic. The recipient opens a smaller gift that contains a note telling the recipient where to find the real package.

Finally, at the end of the evening, the children set their shoes by the fireplace. The shoes are filled with hay and carrots for the horse *Sinterklaas* rides through the streets on St. Nicholas Eve. The children sing a song about how much they hope the cold, wet, foggy weather will not keep *Sinterklaas* away that night. Then they tell their parents how well, or how badly, they have behaved throughout the past year. When well-behaved children awake in the morning, their shoes are filled with nuts, candy, and other surprises.

In the eastern part of Holland, farm families announce the coming of Christmas from the first Sunday of Advent, which is the fourth Sunday before Christmas, until Christmas Eve by blowing a horn made from hollow elder-tree branches. The horns make an eerie noise as they are blown at every farm in the neighborhood.

Later in December, Dutch families decorate a Christmas tree and trim the house with candles, evergreens, and holly. Some children hang up a stocking from the fireplace mantel on Christmas Eve, but there are no more presents after St. Nicholas Day for most Dutch children.

Families go to church together on Christmas Eve and then again on Christmas morning. They gather together for a family dinner of roast hare, venison, goose, or turkey. Eggnog and a mulled drink are specially made for this celebration.

After dinner, the family gathers before the fireplace to tell stories and sing carols.

December 26 is called Second Christmas Day. Often the family goes out to a restaurant to eat on that day. Many concerts, recitals, and other musical performances make this Christmas Day special.

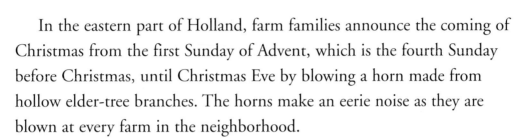

Deck the Halls

Welsh

Don we now our gay ap - par - el, Fa la la la la la la la la la,

Troll the an - cient yule - tide car - ol, Fa la la la la la la la la.

2. See the blazing yule before us,
   Fa la, etc.
   Strike the harp and join the chorus,
   Fa la, etc.
   Follow me in merry measure,
   Fa la, etc.
   While I tell of Christmas treasure.
   Fa la, etc.

3. Fast away the old year passes,
   Fa la, etc.
   Hail the new! ye lads and lasses;
   Fa la, etc.
   Sing we joyous all together,
   Fa la, etc.
   Heedless of the wind and weather.
   Fa la, etc.

I Saw Three Ships

England

1.I saw three ships come sail-ing in, On

2. And what was in those ships all three,
   On Christmas Day, On Christmas Day?
   And what was in those ships all three,
   On Christmas Day in the morning?

3. The Virgin Mary and Christ were there,
   On Christmas Day, On Christmas Day,
   The Virgin Mary and Christ were there,
   On Christmas Day in the morning.

CHRISTMAS IN Australia

Written by Sarah Toast

Illustrated by Robert Y. Larsen and Winky Adam

Australians live on the world's largest island, which is also the world's smallest continent. Most of Australia's immigrants came from England and Ireland, bringing their Christmas customs with them.

Australia is the Land Down Under, where the seasons are opposite to ours. When Australians celebrate Christmas on December 25, it is during summer vacation. Most of Australia is a hot, dry desert, known as the Outback. The grassy or marshy savannas are called the Bush. But most people in Australia live in the green coastal areas of the southwest.

The most popular event of the Christmas season is called Carols by Candlelight. People come together at night to light candles and sing Christmas carols outside. The stars shining above add to the sights and sounds of this wonderful outdoor concert.

Australian families love to do things outside. They love to swim, surf, sail, and ride bicycles. They like to grill meals outdoors on the barbecue, which they call the "barbie."

Families decorate their homes with ferns, palm leaves, and evergreens, along with the colorful flowers that bloom in summer called Christmas bush and Christmas bellflower. Some families put up a Christmas tree. Outdoors, nasturtiums, wisteria, and honeysuckle bloom.

Christmas festivities begin in late November, when schools and church groups present Nativity plays. They sing carols throughout the month of December.

On Christmas Eve, families attend church together. Some children expect Father Christmas to leave gifts, and others wait for Santa Claus to visit and deliver gifts.

After opening presents on Christmas morning, the family sits down to a breakfast of ham and eggs. Then the family goes to church again.

On Christmas Eve in families that observe Irish traditions, the father sets a large candle in a front window of the home to welcome Mary, Joseph, and the Baby Jesus. The youngest child in the family lights the candle. The family goes to midnight mass and attends church on Christmas Day, as well. Afterwards there are parties and festive visits.

Christmas Day is when families and close friends gather together from all over Australia. The highlight of the day is the holiday midday dinner. Some families enjoy a traditional British Christmas dinner of roast turkey or ham and rich plum pudding doused in brandy and set aflame before it is brought to the table. The person who gets the favor baked inside will enjoy good luck all year round.

Other families head for the backyard barbie to grill their Christmas dinner in the sunshine. Many families even go to the beach or to the countryside and enjoy a picnic of cold turkey or ham and a salad. Father Christmas has been known to show up in shorts to greet children at the beach on Christmas!

The day after Christmas, December 26, is Boxing Day. Australians with British and Irish backgrounds leave tips for the grocer, postman, newspaper carrier, and others to thank them for their help in the past year.

New Year's Eve is always a special time, with dinners, dances, and parties. On Twelfth Night, January 6, there is one last party to end the Christmas season.

O Holy Night

Adolphe Adam

We Wish You a Merry Christmas

2. Now bring us some figgy pudding,
   Now bring us some figgy pudding,
   Now bring us some figgy pudding
   And a cup of good cheer!

3. We won't go until we get some,
   We won't go until we get some,
   We won't go until we get some,
   So bring it out here.

Merry Christmas, Everyone!